AUNT AMERICA

Drawings by Joan Berg

Marie Halun Bloch

AUNT
AMERICA

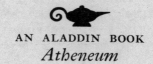

AN ALADDIN BOOK
Atheneum

To Yulia
AND
To the memory of Mihail

Contents

AUNT AMERICA

CHAPTER ONE

An Ordinary Day

The day began like any other for Lesya. She got out of the bed, in the best room, that she shared with her little sister, Anya, and drowsily dressed in the half-light of the early spring morning. In the kitchen, the only other room in the cottage, she greeted Mama and drank a cup of hot tea. There was no milk for the tea. But, as usual, Mamma had cut a generous piece of bread for her.

After breakfast, Lesya stood in front of the mirror in the best room while Mama braided her dark straight hair into two short pigtails. Mama always managed to tie the white ribbon bow on each of Lesya's pigtails so that it looked like a flower behind either ear.

From the mirror Lesya's dark brown eyes gazed moodily back at herself. Her nose seemed to her rather too short. That was because it turned slightly up at the end. Her chin and mouth were soft and tender, like Mama's.

Lesya studied her mother's face, too. She had heard grownups say that Mama had been the prettiest girl in town. That was not easy for Lesya to believe. Though there were not a great many wrinkles on Mama's oval-shaped face, the faded look on it disappeared only when she smiled.

When Mama at last gave her head the final pat, Lesya shouldered her schoolbag and started off. Outside, the sun shone weakly through the morning mist that hovered over the little Ukrainian town. The low hill across the road from their cottage was still a winter brown and the apple trees that grew on it looked dead. It was hard to believe that in May, only two months from now, that hilltop would be a mass of pinkish-white, as festive with blossoms as a bride. To walk within that orchard then was to walk in an other-worldly place.

On the wooden bridge over the stream that

4

threaded its way through the town, Lesya stopped, as she usually did. She hung over the railing and watched chunks of thawing ice bob upon the water as it flowed under the bridge and down the channel meandering across the fields.

Underneath the bridge, between its stone foundation and its floor, was a secret ledge onto which, if you were agile, you could climb and hide from everyone. By hanging your head over the ledge, you could spend an entire afternoon with profit, watching the flow of the water below that was never the same and yet always the same.

Raising her head, Lesya searched the far side of the fields till she saw the great oak of Sweetmeadow. From the bridge, you could see only the top of that venerable oak, far on the other side of town. It grew in the yard of her family's old home.

Others lived there now. It had not belonged to Lesya's family since long before Lesya was born, for much more than her eleven years. Sometimes her wanderings took her past Sweetmeadow, and then she always stared at the house, but without stopping. Three or four families lived in it now. In the front yard shrubs grew wild. But the great oak stood in dignity.

Not far from it was another, even older, oak. It grew in the yard of the wooden church that had been a part of the town since its beginning in the 13th century. The young people, so she had heard grownups say, used to gather under that ancient oak on summer evenings and sing and laugh half the night away. No one ever went there any more. The old church was abandoned, and people nowadays went to the newer church.

"Hey! Lesya!" a voice broke her revery. "You'll be late for school!"

That was Mihail. He thumped across the bridge past her, swinging his schoolbag, and soon disappeared down the road. Lesya scuffed her way slowly along, picking her way around the puddles of melting snow.

She was not fond of school. Only in reading did she ever earn a "5," the highest grade. Her teacher often told her that if she would only get over some of her timidness she would do better. But usually Lesya was content to let other, bolder ones take the lead in class.

6

At school that day Lesya did neither well nor poorly. The times that she kept her mind on what was going on, she did well enough. But more than once, as was her habit, she let her thoughts carry her away from the schoolroom, and then she was startled by the teacher's voice calling her name. As usual, some of the other children snickered at her surprise when she was caught in this way.

It was such an ordinary day that it was almost gone before anything unusual happened. After school that afternoon, Lesya stopped for a bit to play a game of hopscotch with Maria, her best friend.

Lesya had just finished a turn when the town Head came walking up. Though he governed them, he was a stranger among them. He had been named in the first place by some distant authorities as one suited to govern them. Nothing remained then but to elect him. And this had been done.

He sat in his mysterious office in the white building on the square in the middle of town, and rarely appeared on the streets. But suddenly, there he was; and even more surprising, when he came to them, he stopped.

Lesya felt herself stiffening inside. And though Maria kept on playing, Lesya could tell from her movements that she, too, felt ill at ease. Lesya was careful to keep her eyes on the sidewalk, as if she were absorbed in the game.

The Head stood watching for a moment. "Playing hopscotch?" he finally asked.

Though he spoke in Russian, as always, the two girls understood him. For in school, in addition to their native tongue, they had to study Russian, the language of the authorities.

"Da," they replied together in Russian, "we're playing hopscotch."

He turned to Lesya. "You haven't been home yet since school let out?"

A queasy feeling fluttered through Lesya's stomach. She looked straight at the man's face for an instant, to see what was there. He was smiling. "No," she said.

Still smiling, he walked on. Lesya carefully kept her eyes on the sidewalk till she knew he had passed them, and then she turned and stared at his receding back. Why should he ask her a question like that? Why had he smiled?

Why had he spoken to her at all?

Maria suddenly pocketed her hopscotch stone and said, "I'm going home."

And off she flew down the street, the yellow ribbon bow on top of her short brown hair bobbing up and down as she ran.

Lesya turned and ran in the opposite direction. Near the bridge she met Mihail's father. Greeting her, he smiled broadly. Now Lesya slowed to a walk. Why were people smiling at her in such a particular way?

CHAPTER TWO

Letter from America

As Lesya neared her house, she saw her little sister in the yard. Anya must have been watching, for now she let herself out of the gate and came skipping down the road, crying out something as she ran. When she reached Lesya, she flung her little arms around Lesya's middle and piped, "Aunt America coming!"

Lesya laughed. "Oh, you little goose! There's no such person as Aunt America!"

She seized Anya's hand and together they ran through the gate, across the yard, and into the house. As they burst into the kitchen, Lesya was surprised to find two or three of the neighbors there.

And, standing just inside the doorway, was Uncle Vlodko. This was so astounding that Lesya stopped short. Though he was her father's brother and lived nearby, she could not remember that he had ever been in their house. But, of course, that could not be expected.

His round, good-natured face broke into a smile when he saw her. He stretched out his arm and put his hand on her shoulder.

Lesya's father, his tall, lanky frame leaning against the cold stove, was reading from a piece of paper he held in his big rough hand. ". . . I wish you and your families good health, and I kiss you all. Your aunt, Lydia."

A murmur rose from the women sitting on the long benches against the walls, on either side of the kitchen table. When her father looked up, Lesya saw that his thin, pale face had an unusual glow on it; and in his blue eyes, that to Lesya always seemed overcast with an injured look, there was a tender smile.

Mama glanced at Lesya. "An important guest is arriving," she said to her. "Your great aunt, Father's Aunt Lydia."

"From America?" Lesya cried. "Here?"

"In Kiev," Mama replied. "But we'll go there to see her."

"Auntie America!" chirped Anya, dancing about the kitchen.

Lesya laughed and tried to catch her as she danced by. Lesya almost felt like dancing herself, but instead she listened to the grownups.

Granny Katarina, who lived near the square in town, said triumphantly to Mama, "And didn't the cards tell you, not once, but thrice—" She interrupted herself and turned to the woman next to her, "Three times, mind you!—that family from beyond the frontier would come? And you—you only laughed!"

In an unusually gay tone Lesya's mother replied, "And I still laugh, Granny. Fortune-telling is only a pastime."

In a few moments the women arose from the benches, adjusted their head scarves, and, saying goodbye, one by one filed out of the cottage. Immediately after, Uncle Vlodko also took his leave.

Lesya picked up the letter lying on the table. To think that it had found its way from America, all the way across the ocean, precisely to them in this cottage! She pulled the letter out of the envelope. "Dear Nephews, Roman and Vlodko," she read.

As Lesya read on, she was surprised at the unpracticed hand in which the Ukrainian letters were formed. More surprising than this was the misspelling of some of the words; and worst of all, there were even some mistakes in grammar.

Lesya stopped to ask her mother about this. Mama explained that naturally in America Aunt Lydia spoke English most of the time and probably did not get much practice speaking Ukrainian. "But come, Lesya," she went on, "finish the letter and then set the table for supper."

Lesya read on. "At last," Aunt Lydia had written, "I am able to make the journey I have dreamed of for so many years. My beloved family! I am coming to the old country to see you. I shall be coming alone, without my husband or children. Probably I will not be able to visit you at home, but I shall be in Kiev for almost three days, and since that is not far from you, perhaps you can come to me there. I arrive in Kiev on the tenth of April and shall be staying at the Tourist Hotel. I wish you and your families good health, and I kiss you all. Your aunt, Lydia."

After supper that evening, by ones and twos, more people came to their cottage. Word had spread through the town about the marvelous letter from America with its thrilling news. Again and again Lesya's father read it aloud and then let it pass from hand to hand.

As Mihail's father handed the letter back to Father, he said, "My parents—may the earth lie lightly on them—often spoke of your Aunt Lydia and her parents. She was hardly more than an infant when they left for America."

"What a long time ago that was!" Father exclaimed. "Before the First World War."

"Those days, so they say, were not much better than these," Mihail's father went on. "But at least anyone who had the wish and the money could leave. Nowadays, my friends, our frontier is a prison wall." He gave a short laugh. "If they should open it, overnight we would all leave." A merry look lit his eyes. "For that matter, even the dogs would follow us!"

The grownups rocked with laughter.

Antin spoke up. "But if we were masters of our own land, now, who would care to leave it?"

Mama's hand flew to her lips. "Please. No more," she murmured. "Someone may be listening under the window."

Lesya stared at her father. Uncle Vlodko, she thought to herself, would never have allowed such talk in his house.

Antin sat drumming his long slim fingers on the table as if he were fingering the strings of his bandura. "My older brother, the one who works on the docks at Odessa, was home not long ago," he went on in a hoarse whisper. "He told us that they have been loading canned meat and canned milk on ships for Africa."

The grownups seemed stirred by this news.

Antin went on. "The world thinks, 'Ach! How rich those devils are, to be able to spare so much food!' But which of our children has had milk since early winter? Tell me!"

"Please!" Mama begged. "No more!"

Anastasia, who had been sitting silent next to Mama, rose to go. "My infant," she murmured. "I must go to him."

Mama saw her to the door. "When do you plan to christen him?" she asked.

A smile lit Anastasia's pretty young face. "Soon," she said, and hurried out.

The letter lay on the table as if forgotten. Quietly Lesya picked it up again. This time she examined the envelope. It was addressed both in English and Ukrainian to her father. Probably Aunt Lydia had addressed the letter to him only because he was older than Uncle Vlodko. Perhaps she did not realize how important Uncle Vlodko was.

Lesya looked at the English words on the envelope for a long time, wondering how they were pronounced. Across the top were two, *air mail,* but though she knew the sound of each letter, she did not know how to pronounce them or what they meant.

All the while Lesya dawdled over the envelope, she was filled with the delicious knowledge that she would find a treat inside it whenever she chose to take the letter out and read it again. She turned the envelope over and examined the back of it. She could tell that the censor, having opened and read the letter, had not

17

bothered to repaste the flap neatly. There was really no need for neatness.

At last, unable to put it off any longer, Lesya pulled out the letter and began to read it, slowly this time, savoring every word. She did not notice that all the guests had finally left until she heard Mama say, "Put the letter away now, Lesya. It's past your bedtime."

"Mama, just let me finish," Lesya begged. "I'm right in the middle of it."

Father laughed. "By now, haven't you learned it by heart?"

Lesya smiled. That was true. She got up and went into the best room. As she prepared for bed, she stopped to search for a certain photograph among the group that hung on the wall. When she found it, she looked at it for a long time.

It was a picture of Aunt Lydia in America, when she was about the same age as Lesya now. She had straight blonde hair, like Uncle Vlodko's, combed back from her face and reaching to her shoulders. Her face was shaped like Father's, oval, with high cheekbones and a high brow.

18

In her arms the little girl held a black puppy. From infancy Lesya had known the curious name of the dog—Pepper. The picture had been taken out-of-doors. The girl stood under a tree, and behind her was a house, the front door of which stood invitingly open. Whenever Lesya's eyes had come to that door, she had wondered what was inside. Now Aunt Lydia was coming, and she, Lesya, could ask her, personally.

Just as Lesya was crawling into bed, Mama came into the room. "You haven't said good-night to your father, Lesya," she said gently.

Mama said this every night, and Lesya always dreaded it. But every night she did as she did now. Dutifully she went into the kitchen, where her father sat on the bench, and gave him a hug and a kiss. Father's eyes always lighted up when she did this, and the injured look in them almost disappeared.

Duty done, Lesya climbed into bed beside her little sister and snuggled under the plump feather quilt that rose so high over her that she could see only the ceiling of the moonlit room. Her parents, as usual, lay down to sleep on the long benches in the kitchen.

Anya was already fast asleep. But for Lesya
sleep would not come. For a long time she wondered and thought about Aunt America. In the
dark, she smiled to have caught herself thinking
of her aunt by the name Anya had made up.
Well, Aunt America it would be, then!

And what would her aunt be like? America
was a rich country, people said. Would her
aunt, then, be wearing silks and satins, and perhaps a long fur coat like the Head's wife, and
an elegant hat with feathers on it, like the one
great-aunt Natalya wore in the picture on the
wall?

Wouldn't it be delicious if the authorities allowed Aunt America to visit them right here at
home? Then Lesya would show her the great
oak of Sweetmeadow and the school. Lesya
wriggled deeper under the quilt. That was not
even to be thought of; they never let foreigners
visit here. Foreigners were allowed to visit only
certain of the big cities, like Kiev.

An anxious thought now came to Lesya. Did
Aunt America know about Father and Mama?
When she learned that Father, and even Mama,
had been in prison, how would she feel about

that? Would she feel ashamed?

Lesya tried never to think of it. But sometimes, like now, she couldn't help herself. She had been only four when the authorities took away her parents. Once again, she heard the sudden pounding on the door in the darkness of the night, and the hard, strangers' voices of the men who had come striding into the cottage, filling every least corner of it with their presence.

She easily remembered the moment when they had taken her parents out of the cottage, and the stillness afterwards. She clearly remembered even her feelings. She had felt that her father, for some grownup reason that surely had nothing to do with her, had abandoned her. This had filled her with such terror that she had not even been able to cry.

Aunt Sophia had appeared then, her face sternly set, and had bundled her in the quilt and carried her in her arms through the black, evil night to the warm safety of her own house. And there Lesya had lived, with Aunt Sophia and Uncle Vlodko and her young cousin, Elena.

No one had ever spoken to Lesya about the reason for her parents' absence. But sometimes at night, when they thought she was asleep beside Elena on the bed in the best room, she used to listen anxiously to the conversation of the grownups in the next room for some word of her parents.

Often she was rewarded and, piecing together what she heard, she learned that her father, and her mother, too, had been suspected of some activity with those secret ones who worked to make Ukraine a free nation. They were by no means the only ones who had been taken away.

Lesya learned, too, that while Aunt Sophia had nothing but kind words for her parents, Uncle Vlodko sometimes seemed scornful of them. "Look at me," he often declared. "I keep my mind on my own business, which is to look after my family, and I stay away from those who want to stir up needless trouble."

Lesya admired him for that.

The day Lesya had started school, Aunt Sophia had taken her aside and carefully warned her about her conduct. "You must never repeat what you may have overheard a grownup say. Do you understand, Lesya?"

Staring up at Aunt Sophia's anxious, kindly

face, Lesya had understood. After that she had always been careful not to attract attention to herself, nor show any particular emotion, nor be the first to offer her friendship to anyone. Aunt Sophia was a good teacher.

Then three years ago Mama and Father had come back. For a long time after, people had shunned them, spoke to them only casually, and never came to the house. It was like school, Lesya thought—people were kind but careful. Only after a while had the bolder ones begun to visit them now and again. Then, after a longer time, during which nothing had happened to these, even a few of the more timid had begun to come.

Until this very day, however, Uncle Vlodko had never come. And how could you blame him? If he should seem too friendly with his brother, he would risk losing his good job and perhaps face even worse dangers. Surely everyone understood that. It was enough, Lesya thought, that he had taken care of her. Even that had been a danger.

Thank goodness for Uncle Vlodko! Aunt America could not fail to be impressed with the fact that he had a good job that kept his hands soft and white and that he always got on well with the authorities.

Aunt America was sure to like him.

CHAPTER THREE

On the Eve

The very next day, on the way to school, Lesya noticed the difference the letter had made. Grownups who ordinarily just nodded to her now smiled broadly as they passed. Everyone in town knew about the letter.

On the way, Mihail and some of his cronies fell in with Lesya, but casually, as if they had not in fact been lingering in wait for her. Although she knew quite well it was the letter that intrigued them, to tease them she began to chatter away about the history lesson that had been assigned.

Finally, unable to stand it any longer, Mihail burst out, "But is it true that you have an aunt coming from America on a visit?"

At this, they all stopped and gazed at her as if everything depended on her answer. "Of course it's true!" she said.

"But what exactly did she say in her letter?" Mihail persisted.

"Only that she is coming. But you can come over and read it for yourself if you want."

Julie and her brother Petro came along then, and Lesya skipped on ahead with Julie. As they approached the schoolhouse, near the square, Lesya saw that a large group of children were clustered about someone. When Lesya joined them, she saw that they were all listening to her cousin Elena.

This did not surprise Lesya. Elena enjoyed being the center of attention. She was talking with a certain air, as if she herself, single-handedly, had managed the miracle that was about to happen. The dimples at the corners of her strong, wide mouth now deepened, now disappeared as she talked about the letter, about Aunt Lydia, and about their plans to see her in Kiev.

As Lesya watched, she wondered why some people were so lucky. Elena could talk with ease to people; she lived in a house better than most; she wore better clothes; and, as if that were not enough, she had Uncle Vlodko for her father.

In her thoughts, Lesya never dared go further. For of all sins, the most wicked was not to love your own father.

That day, as if the teacher, too, were fascinated by the letter from America, she paid particular attention to Lesya and called on her to recite more often than usual. When Lesya stood up, everyone gazed on her and hung on her words as if she, herself, were some marvelous creature from afar who was speaking words of rare wisdom. Lesya could hardly bear it.

When school was at last over, Maria walked part way home with Lesya. "You'll be going to Kiev, too, when your aunt comes, won't you?" Maria asked.

Lesya smiled happily and nodded.

Maria had been to Kiev, not once, but two or three times, and she had often told Lesya about it. Maria had seen the ancient Golden Gates of Kiev. She had seen the Pecherska

27

Monastery, which hundreds of years ago had been a great center of Ukrainian art and book learning. And she had even been in the nearby Catacombs in the bluff along the river, where they used to bury people a long time ago. Now, for perhaps the hundredth time, Lesya asked her to tell about it all once more.

Maria sighed, but in her good-natured way, she began. "It's a big city," she said. "And the sidewalks in the center of the town are crowded with people. On Khreshchatik Street there is a big department store, filled with all kinds of things."

"Tell me about the toys," Lesya prompted.

And Maria, knowing quite well what she meant, obligingly replied, "There are dolls of all kinds. One, I remember, could open and close her eyes."

Lesya sighed. She had never owned a doll. Now, of course, being past eleven years old, she was too big for one. Still . . .

"On the street near the Golden Gates is a tree," Maria went on, "and in the tree, ravens nest." She put her hands over her ears and rocked her head. "*Okh,* you should hear their

28

cawing! What a racket!"

Lesya gazed off into the distance. When Aunt Lydia came, she would at last see the wonders of Kiev for herself! And who could tell what good things might happen there?

At home, in the days that followed, people continued to come, by ones and twos, to examine the letter and read it and discuss it, word by word. Time and again, Aunt Lydia's picture was taken off the wall and passed from hand to hand. Soon everyone knew that she had once had a dog and that its curious name had been "Pepper."

Granny Katarina told it all over town, to everyone who would listen, that her fortune-telling cards had predicted ("Not once, but thrice, mind you!") that a beloved guest would come from beyond the frontier. Some were awed by this strange power of the cards and some, like Lesya's mother, merely laughed and called it pure chance.

Everyone in town shared the family's joy and wonder over Aunt Lydia's coming. It was as if she belonged to all of them! The few days of her stay in Kiev were going to be like a great

29

holiday, like Easter or Christmas or a wedding of bygone days.

Then one day when Lesya came home from school, something strange happened. When she came in, she found the kitchen empty. But voices were coming from the other room. She stood and listened and could not believe her ears. For, besides the voices of Mama and Father, she thought she recognized that of the Head. "And are you having enough milk?" she heard him ask.

Lesya glanced into the other room through the open door. The Head was sitting on a chair, his large, flat face oddly flushed with an expression of good will. Mama sat on the edge of the divan and Father, smoking a rare cigarette, was leaning against the table on which Mama kept her house plants. There was a curious expression on his face. In his eyes, amusement glinted.

The Head repeated the question.

Father leisurely blew out the smoke before answering. "I heard you the first time," he replied casually, in Ukrainian. Then, suddenly raising his voice, he said, "And what kind of idiocy are you indulging in now? You know as

well as I that I've had to sell my cow for lack of feed, that there isn't milk to be bought in the commissary, and that my children have been doing without—along with the others. Where am I to go for milk? Africa?"

Lesya's heart leaped in fright. Her hand flew to her mouth. Surely that was no way to speak to an authority? It was dangerous! What would they do to Father now? Why couldn't he behave the way Uncle Vlodko did?

Panic-stricken, Lesya turned to run out of the cottage. But now the Head was speaking. Her heart pounding, she stopped to listen. The Head could not have understood everything Father had said, for his tone was mild.

"Now, now, no need to get angry, my friend," he said. "Go to the commissary. I'll leave orders for them to sell you milk. And how about meat? Do you have enough?"

After the Head had left the cottage and was delicately picking his way down the road, muddy with the spring thaw, Lesya's parents stood looking at each other for a long moment. Then they burst into hilarious laughter. Father laughed so hard he finally had to wipe tears from his eyes.

Lesya stood staring at them, half in fear, not knowing what to make of this strange behavior.

Father seized Lesya and swung her around. "Blessings on my Aunt Lydia!" he cried. "Thanks to her visit, my children shall have milk!"

That was Father's way of looking at it. Uncle Vlodko would have pointed out how thoughtful and generous the Head was.

That night at supper Mama poured milk into large glasses for Lesya and her sister. "Enjoy it while you can, children," she said.

At first, Lesya sipped the milk gingerly, as if it were something distasteful. Then, along with Anya, she ended with drinking not one glass, but two.

Over supper Mama and Father discussed plans for their journey to Kiev. Since they could not afford to stay in a hotel, they would have to come home each night. Not even Uncle Vlodko could afford a hotel room.

It was decided that Anya would not go with them, for Aunt Sophia had insisted that she would be glad to stay at home and look after the child one day. Mama and Father and Lesya, Uncle Vlodko and Elena would go to Kiev on Saturday, the first day of Aunt Lydia's visit. Then, the next day Mama would stay at home so that Aunt Sophia could go.

Father got permission to be absent from his work on the government farm. Since school kept on Saturdays, he wrote a note asking that Lesya be excused, also.

Now Lesya began counting the days in earnest. At last there were three, then two, then only one day before the great event.

Getting ready for bed that night, Lesya washed with special care over the basin in the kitchen. Then she laid out the slipover sweater that was her best and that she wore only on the most important occasions. Part of it was blue, but the top part was white and dotted with shiny metal spangles. Unfortunately, some of the spangles were missing. Her best cotton dress was a little too short. But Mama had washed it, and it was fresh. Mama was even allowing her to wear her best hair ribbons, a pair of bright blue ones with shiny satin on one side.

For hours that night Lesya tossed and turned and could not sleep. Was Aunt America thinking of them, too, tonight, and of their meeting tomorrow? Would she notice Lesya's spangled sweater and her new hair ribbons? Perhaps not. Perhaps Aunt America had many dresses that were spangled all over.

Again Lesya wondered what Aunt Lydia would think of them all. One thing was certain:

she would like Uncle Vlodko. And then—who knew? When Father saw that, perhaps he would try to be more like him.

Then there was Kiev to think of. The promise of being in the capital city of Ukraine was thrilling, but it was a little frightening, too. What if she should get lost?

Ach! There were so many things to think about! But Lesya at last drifted off to sleep.

Once, sometime during the night, she awoke and listened to an airplane flying overhead. "Maybe Aunt Lydia is on that plane," she thought hazily.

Then she turned over and fell contentedly asleep again.

CHAPTER FOUR

To Kiev!

It was still dark the next morning when Lesya and her parents walked to the square and got on the earliest autobus for Kiev. The bus was filled with townspeople taking produce they had grown, on the small plots alloted them for their own use, to sell in the city market. Almost everyone held a basket of winter apples on his lap.

Uncle Vlodko and Elena, who had arrived first, had saved three seats. Everyone smiled knowingly as Lesya and her parents walked down the aisle.

While they waited for the autobus to start, Lesya sat in a cloud of dreams. She could not decide which of the exciting things that were about to happen that very day was the more exciting: to meet an aunt from faraway America, or to be visiting Kiev for the first time.

Suddenly the public radio on the square began to blare for the day. That meant that it was six o'clock and soon the autobus would start. Lesya roused, yawned, and sat up straight. The bus conductor, a young girl in a frayed quilted jacket, got on; and when she had collected the fares, at last they started off. It was already broad daylight.

For many miles they passed rolling fields still bare of plants. Lesya watched the thin veils of early morning mist swirl up off the ground and disappear in the growing warmth of the sunshine.

Now and again they passed through a village. The clusters of cottages, like setting hens, nestled cozily upon the earth. The walls of some were painted a sharp, ugly blue, streaked by rain. Some of the roofs were thatched. Pitched steeply, they ended in eaves that hung low over the small casement windows, giving the cottages a secret, shadowy look. This al-

37

ways reminded Lesya of the picture of great-aunt Natalya, taken on her wedding trip to Vienna long ago. In it she was wearing a great plumed hat that cast a mysterious shadow over her eyes.

The houses were so much like those at home that Lesya did not give them a second glance. After a long time, they began to pass many people, all streaming toward a large, two-story, brick building surrounded by a high wire fence. It was a factory.

Then Mama, sitting beside her, pointed through the window. "Look, Lesya, we are crossing the Dniepro River," she said.

All her life Lesya had heard about the Dniepro, and sometimes at school she had read about it. Looking up the river as they rumbled over the wide bridge, Lesya could see that it wound in a broad, majestic curve across the flat land.

Her father leaned over from the seat behind. "Look on top of that high bluff ahead of us, Lesya. You will see the spire and cupolas of Pecherska Monastery. Quick, look!"

Lesya turned her eyes toward the front windows of the autobus and there, on the bluff toward which they were riding, she saw a cluster of cupolas glinting gold in the morning sun. Then they disappeared.

The autobus began to climb a steep, winding street to the top of the bluff. At last, at the curb of a broad avenue, it came to a stop. As everyone quietly got off, again they smiled.

Lesya held tightly to Mama's hand while they crossed the wide street. On the corner to which they crossed stood the big department store Maria had told her about, where the dolls were.

The wide sidewalk they were walking along was crowded with people. Lesya had never seen so many all at once. And the odd thing was that they all acted like strangers to each other. At home, most people knew each other and exchanged greetings.

Most of the people wore city clothes. And now Father, with his high boots into which his trousers were tucked, with his shabby felt jacket and black cap, suddenly looked out of place.

They came to a large knot of people, mostly men, standing before a high window, intently

watching a chess board hung so that all could
see the chessmen. Mama explained that the
match was being played elsewhere, but the
moves were made also on this board so that
people could follow the game. As they were
working their way through the crowd, a groan
went up. Evidently one of the players had made
a bad move. Both Uncle Vlodko and Father
kept their eyes on the board until they had
passed it.

At last, a little farther on, they stopped in
front of a tall, plain building. On a plaque on
the front of it, Lesya read, "Tourist Hotel."
Her heart began to pound. Somewhere within
this building was Aunt Lydia.

The grownups consulted. It was decided that
Uncle Vlodko would be the one to ask for Aunt
Lydia. For one thing, he was dressed in city
fashion, and Father was not. And for another
—well, it could not be denied that he knew how
to deal with officials.

Uncle Vlodko led the way through the doors
into the hotel. On the left of the little lobby
was a stand where books and cards were sold.
Directly ahead of them was a large cage with

a wrought iron door. To the right of it, a narrow flight of stairs led to the upper floors.

With a matter-of-fact air that Lesya thought was very impressive, Uncle Vlodko pressed a button beside the cage door. A tall thin man, with a sour expression on his face, appeared from somewhere. When Uncle Vlodko gave him Aunt Lydia's name, he nodded, opened the cage door, and wordlessly waited for them to file in. Then he himself squeezed into the cage, closed the gate, pushed a lever, and the cage began to move upward.

In a moment it came to a halt, and the man opened the door onto a narrow corridor. In front of them stood a desk. A handsome, buxom, dark-haired woman sitting at the desk looked them over appraisingly as they were filing out. Before they had even approached her, she asked pleasantly in Russian, "What do you wish?"

Uncle Vlodko worked his way to the front of their little group, stepped smartly forward, took off his hat, and said in Russian, "If you please, we have come to see a relative."

"Name?" the woman asked, not taking her

eyes off him.

Uncle Vlodko pulled Aunt Lydia's letter out of his coat pocket, stepped forward, and laid it on the desk. Then he stepped back and waited while the woman leisurely read the things written on the envelope. At last she looked up, her dark eyebrows arched, and handed the letter back. "Madame is necessary to you?" she asked.

Lesya glanced up at Mama. What did this mean, *necessary? Necessary* did not at all describe the incredulous joy of Aunt Lydia's coming to them from the other side of the world, nor the weeks of anxious waiting for this very moment.

Uncle Vlodko nodded, and repeated the Russian word. "Necessary, if you please."

"I shall find out," the woman said, "whether Madame is able to see you. She may be resting or otherwise engaged."

Again Lesya looked up at her mother. Aunt Lydia had written them that she was coming especially to see them. What, then, could now engage her so much as to prevent this? When she glanced at Father, she saw amusement flicker in his eyes. At a time like this!

The woman turned to the telephone on her desk, lifted the receiver, and spoke into it. After a pause, she said, "Madame? Some relatives have arrived to see you." Another pause, then, "Very well."

Leisurely she replaced the receiver, turned to Uncle Vlodko, and said, "Madame is disengaged and will see you. Follow this corridor to the right, to room number seven." She smiled as she spoke, but somehow the smile chilled Lesya.

As they walked along the dim corridor, Uncle Vlodko and Elena in front, Lesya could feel the look of the woman on her back. She had all she could do to keep from turning around. Hunching her shoulders to make herself as small as possible, she walked with shaking knees between her parents. Father's hand, icy cold, squeezed hers so tight it almost hurt. She pulled it free.

They came at last to a turn in the corridor, and around the turn someone stood silhouetted by the dim light coming through a window at the end.

A soft voice called out, "Roman? Vlodko?"

43

It was Aunt Lydia.

Uncle Vlodko reached her first. He enveloped her in his arms and kissed each of her cheeks. As he stepped away, Lesya saw there were tears in his eyes.

As Father stepped forward, his arms outspread, a hoarse cry suddenly burst from his lips. It frightened Lesya. Weeping aloud, Father held Aunt Lydia in his arms. Lesya was shocked through and through. Never, even in the worst of times, had she heard her father weep. But Aunt Lydia was weeping, too.

Mama stepped forward and laid a gentle hand on Father's shoulder. "Enough," she said. "Enough. They'll hear . . . It isn't well . . ."

At last Father came to himself. He stepped aside and drew Mama forward. "Aunt Lydia," he whispered. "This is my wife."

Mama and Aunt Lydia looked into each other's eyes for an instant and then quietly embraced. Elena was crowding forward. Aunt Lydia stooped and smiled through her tears. "And this . . .?"

"I'm Elena, Auntie," she spoke up, giving her aunt a hearty hug.

44

Lesya hung back, watching. But now Father took her hand and led her forward. "And this must be Lesya?" Auntie said.

Lesya was suddenly so overcome with shyness that she could not speak. But words were not needed. She felt herself gathered into her aunt's arms and held tight. Aunt Lydia smelled delicately of perfume, not the flowery kind that was sold at the commissary at home, but something spicy and heady.

Aunt Lydia stood up and took her hand. "Come into my room," she said, leading the way.

CHAPTER FIVE

In the Park

Lesya did not know what to look at first, her
aunt or the grand room into which she
had led them. The floor was covered
with a rug splattered with large red flowers.
Lesya would have hesitated to step on it, but
Aunt Lydia led the way right across it to an
upholstered divan. With Lesya and Elena on
either side of her, she sat down.

When they were all seated, Uncle Vlodko
spoke. "Well, and how does our Kiev please
you?"

Aunt Lydia looked at him soberly. "I just
arrived late yesterday afternoon. And it was
not Kiev I came to see, but you."

Now Lesya had the courage to look straight

at Aunt Lydia. Though there were white hairs
among the light brown, there was scarcely a
wrinkle on her face. Except when she smiled.
Then lines fanned out across the temples and
her blue eyes became slits.

The most startling thing about Aunt Lydia
was her thinness. Perhaps she had been ill? But
her voice, though soft, was strong. She did not
act weak from hunger, either. On the contrary,
unlike Mama and Father and Uncle Vlodko,
who were subdued in manner, she was vivacious.

"Aunt Lydia!" Father was now speaking.
"We could not write you everything. Did you
know that they put me in prison? And my wife,
too?"

Lesya looked at her father in dismay. He had
spoken of the one thing she thought he would
never mention. She glanced at Aunt Lydia. Her
aunt had leaned forward, a serious look on
her face.

Uncle Vlodko, frowning, had begun to fidget
in his chair. Mama glanced at him and suddenly
stood up. Looking significantly at Father, she
said loudly, "It's such a beautiful day. The sun
is shining outdoors, and here we all sit cooped

up. Perhaps Aunt Lydia would like to see some of our beautiful parks in Kiev. The children," she declared, "are getting restless!"

Lesya was startled at this. She wasn't feeling restless at all. And at first Father looked surprised at this unseemly interruption. Then, as if he understood something, he stood up.

Aunt Lydia seemed to be just as puzzled by this behavior as Lesya was. But without asking questions, she stood up, walked to the big wardrobe in a corner of the room, and took out her coat.

Outside the hotel, Mama said, "It is not well to speak of private matters in a public place. Walls may have ears."

Aunt Lydia glanced at her, and a look of understanding came into her eyes. But, pressing her lips firmly together, she said nothing.

Turning to the right, they started out, Lesya and Elena on either side of their aunt. When they reached the corner, Uncle Vlodko led them to the right. "There's a nice little park not far down this street," he said.

The sidewalks were thronged. All eyes looked first at Aunt Lydia, then swiftly over the rest

of them, then back at Aunt Lydia. Everyone
knew she was a foreigner.

It was her aunt's clothes that attracted the
looks, Lesya decided. For, though Aunt Lydia
was not dressed in silk and satin after all, her
clothes were unmistakably foreign. Especially
her shoes. Instead of the broad-toed, thick-
heeled oxfords, which were Mama's best, Aunt
Lydia was wearing dainty shoes with such slim
heels that Lesya wondered why they did not
snap in two.

But perhaps after all it was not only the
clothes. There was something about the way
Aunt Lydia carried herself that made you look
at her.

At first Lesya was bursting with pride that
all should look at them, and perhaps envy them
for knowing a foreigner. But after a time so
much notice seemed too much.

She looked up at her aunt's face to see
whether she, too, was bothered by the stares.
As if she felt the look, Aunt Lydia glanced
down and smiled. The smile sent a warm glow
through Lesya.

"Lesya!" her aunt said. "What a beautiful

name! Were you named after Lesya Ukrainka, the poet?"

"Yes, Auntie," Lesya answered with a shy smile. She had not thought it a great thing before, but now all at once her name took on new importance.

At that moment, from her left she heard raucous cries. She looked across the street, and there she saw a tree whose bare branches were draped with big, shaggy nests. Great black birds were hopping from branch to branch and keeping up a hoarse cawing. Ravens! Maria had been quite right about them.

Then, just a little farther on, they passed the Golden Gates of Kiev. In the history book at school, an old picture showed them surrounded by cottages. Now there were apartment houses all around. There was nothing golden about the gates any longer, either; for during the long wars against the Tatars, in the distant past, the enemy had stripped off the gold and stolen it away.

The park he had in mind, Uncle Vlodko now said, was only two blocks farther. In the next moment, on the same street, but on the other

side, Lesya caught sight of a cupola reaching gracefully into the clear blue of the sky, its gold blazing in the sun. Aunt Lydia must have noticed it at the same time, for she gave a delighted cry, "St. Sophia Cathedral!"

As Lesya looked up at the cupola, she felt thrilled. At last, with her own eyes, she was seeing this monument of history that she felt she had known from the day she was born. As they passed, Lesya could see golden clusters of other cupolas on buildings within the Cathedral grounds. She yearned to go inside. But they walked on.

Just past the Cathedral, they came at last to
the park they were looking for. Opposite it, in
a little green space in the middle of the broad
street, stood a great bronze statue of a man on
a rearing horse.

Elena looked up at Aunt Lydia and said, "That's Bohdan Khmelnitzky, Auntie. But perhaps you do not know about him? If not, I will tell you. He was—"

Aunt Lydia smiled. "But I do know, Elena. He was the Ukrainian statesman of the 17th century."

Just as they started into the park, a photographer came up to them and asked whether they wanted their picture taken. A delighted smile lit his face when Aunt Lydia replied that they would. "You are from America, perhaps?" he asked. "But you speak our tongue without a trace of accent!"

"From America," she replied. "Ukrainian was my parents' tongue, and I learned from them. Now, let's see, shall we have St. Sophia for a background, or Bohdan? Let's have one of each."

"Ah! St. Sophia!" the photographer exclaimed. "An ancient handiwork of our people! A thousand years old!"

As they grouped themselves for the pictures, Aunt Lydia made sure that Lesya, as well as Elena, stood next to her. After she had paid

54

the photographer and made arrangements for him to bring the finished pictures to the hotel, they went farther into the park. There they found an empty bench that was long enough for all six of them.

Grandmothers were wheeling their infant grandchildren in strollers back and forth along the walks. Nearby, there was a small playground where older children were playing. There were teeter-tauters and a jungle gym and some swings. Lesya wanted to play in the playground, for there was none at home. But, she supposed, she was too big for that. And besides, she would rather stay with Aunt Lydia.

"The authorities," Father was saying, "thought we were engaged in some kind of underground activity. We—"

Uncle Vlodko interrupted with an angry exclamation. "And weren't you? Why don't you behave yourself? Look at me," he continued, "I tend to my work, bother nobody—"

Father broke in, looking steadily at Uncle Vlodko, "Isn't it more accurate to say that you bother *about* nobody?"

Lesya wished now she had gone to the playground. How could Father say such things?

But why, she wondered next, did Uncle Vlodko flush at the words?

A troubled look came into Aunt Lydia's eyes. "Please," she said. "Please! How can you quarrel? Don't you have enough enemies, both of you, without making enemies of each other?"

Father and Uncle Vlodko stared grimly off into the distance, until one of the grannies came strolling by. Then Father suddenly turned his attention to her. "Eh, Granny!" he called out. "Mind the child! Don't you see the sun is shining right in its eyes? Do you want its eyesight ruined?"

The old woman chuckled. "Ach!" she cried good-humoredly as she stopped to lower the buggy hood, "and what do you know about it?"

Father smiled and winked at Lesya. "I'm a specialist!" he cried.

That cleared away the anger. Aunt Lydia looked down at Lesya and said, "Why don't you and Elena go and play on the swings for a bit? It must be dull for you to sit here like this."

Silently Lesya thanked her aunt as she and Elena slid off the bench and ran to the playground. Luckily, two of the swings were empty. Two were occupied by little ones whose fathers were pushing them and talking to each other.

Though Lesya had never before been on a swing, without being shown she knew how to pump herself up. Soon she was swinging high into the sky. As she swung backwards, she caught snatches of the conversation between the two men.

". . . seized at the border . . ." The rest faded as Lesya swung away forward.

". . . letters in his luggage . . ." Again she went sweeping away.

". . . did they do to the fellow?"

What a joy it was to fly, free as a bird! Elena, too, was delighted. "Next time I come to Kiev," she cried, "I'm going to spend all of my time in this park!"

As Lesya swooped high into the air and down again, the reality of Aunt America's being right there with them was so delicious that she could hardly bear the feeling inside her. It filled her so full she wanted to shout joy to the skies.

All too soon she heard Mama's soft voice calling. Just one more swing, and then, for good

measure, just one more, and she leaped off.
With Elena, she ran back to the grownups. Aunt
America was standing now, and Elena, evidently feeling just as Lesya did, flung her arms
around her aunt's waist. Lesya looked on and
smiled. Elena had done just what she, Lesya,
would have liked to do.

Aunt America laughed and then took hold
of Lesya's hand. Why, Lesya thought, she knew
just how I felt.

"So you two have been enjoying yourselves?"
Aunt America said. "Come now, we will go
back to the hotel for lunch. And then," she
said, turning to the grownups, "I may have a
surprise for all of you."

CHAPTER SIX

The Doll

Back in the hotel room, Lesya watched her aunt's every move. First she telephoned to the restaurant below. Presently a waitress came. Then Aunt Lydia sat on the sofa with Elena on one side and Lesya on the other. Together they looked over the long menu the waitress brought.

Lesya had not dreamed there was so much food in the world as was listed on that menu. Many of the dishes were unfamiliar to her. But soon she saw something she especially liked. "Compote!" she cried. "They have fruit compote!"

Auntie smiled. "Would you like some then, for dessert?"

Soon after the waitress had left, Aunt Lydia got up and went to her suitcase, which was lying on a bench. As she delved into it, she said, "I've brought something for you children."

Lesya slid to the edge of the divan and waited. At last Aunt Lydia drew something out of the suitcase.

It was a doll.

"Ooh!" Elena exclaimed.

Lesya held her breath.

"This is for you, Elena," Aunt Lydia said.

Lesya let out her breath. Never in all her life had she seen such a beautiful doll. Elena ran from the sofa and took it. By way of thanks, she gave her aunt a big hug.

Aunt Lydia turned back to the suitcase. "And this—" she began, rummaging in the suitcase again.

"Oh, please, please," Lesya silently prayed, "let it be a doll! I know I'm too big for one. But all the same, just this once, let it be a doll!"

In her hand, Aunt America was holding a book. Her eyes were shining. "And this is for you, Lesya, dear."

Tears welled into Lesya's eyes. Somehow

she managed to take the book, and somehow she managed to murmur, "Thank you, Auntie."

Somehow she managed to walk back to the sofa, where she sat with her head down so no one would see her tears.

Through them she saw the name of the book on her lap, "Ukrainian Folk Tales." On the snow-white cover was a picture in rich colors. One part of her said that the book was beautiful, and reminded her that she had never owned a book in all her life. This part of her also told her that it was plain to see Auntie thought it a valuable gift.

But the other part of her almost sobbed aloud with despair. To have come so close to owning a doll! Her chest felt all raw inside, as if she had been wounded.

Aunt Lydia seemed to sense that something was wrong, for now she sat down beside Lesya and put her arm around her shoulders. This only brought Lesya to the edge of disaster. Her throat ached with tears and for an anxious moment she wasn't sure that she could hold them back. But after a moment the danger passed.

Luckily the waitress soon returned, bearing

an enormous tray laden with their lunch.
Though a large pitcher of milk stood in the
center of the table, and the pirohi, little dump-
lings filled with meat, were Lesya's favorite
food, which she seldom had, she was not hungry
now. It was truly a banquet, but try as she
would, she could not eat.

Toward the end of the meal, Aunt America
glanced at her watch. "It's time," she said, ris-
ing. "Please excuse me. I have an appointment
with the tourist bureau here in the hotel. I
won't be long."

With her aunt gone, Lesya began to feel a
little better. The grownups talked quietly among
themselves, but Lesya did not listen. Elena was
absorbed in her doll. Lesya excused herself and
went into the bathroom, which she had noticed
when they first came into the room. There she
looked carefully around.

On a shelf next to the washbowl were a va-
riety of intriguing things. Though ordinarily
Lesya would not have dreamed of touching any
of them, curiosity about these American things
now overpowered her. The toothbrush was in
a box of its own that looked like glass, for you

could see right through it. But when you squeezed it, unlike glass, it bent.

A tall bottle filled with dark greenish-brown liquid stood beside it. Lesya unscrewed the top and sniffed the contents. The heady smell of Aunt America filled her nose, and for a moment the wounded feeling in her chest came back full strength. Lesya had been ready to love Aunt Lydia even before she saw her, but now— Struggling to swallow the tears that were filling her throat again, Lesya tipped the bottle over onto her sweater and watched the perfume trickle out through the tiny hole in the top.

Now she noticed a pair of shoes on the floor, like the ones Aunt Lydia was wearing except that they were dark blue. She was just about to take off her own shoes to try them on, when she heard excited exclamations coming from the grownups.

Lesya retied the laces of her own shoes and returned to the other room. The grownups were all standing with unbelieving, joyous expressions on their faces. Uncle Vlodko seemed to be recovering from some sort of surprise and, having done so, began in a loud voice to make a formal statement, as if he were addressing strangers from a platform. "Indeed," he pronounced, "it is most kind of the authorities to grant you the privilege of visiting us in our town."

At this, Father's look of joy changed to one of irritation, and Aunt America looked at Uncle Vlodko as if he had said something foolish. He glanced away.

Mama, seeing Lesya, held out her arms to her. "Just think, Lesya, Aunt Lydia has received permission to come home with us!"

"For today and tomorrow!" Elena cried.

"A marvel!" Father murmured.

It was a marvel, Lesya thought. Whether she liked her aunt or not made no difference now. What did that matter, when such an important event was about to happen?

For one thing, while Aunt Lydia was with them at home, perhaps Lesya would have a chance to ask about some of the things she had always wondered about. Then, too,—and this was most important of all—Aunt Lydia was going to see for herself Uncle Vlodko's fine house and the good way he lived. Lesya's face lighted up as she looked at her aunt.

Aunt Lydia's coming home with them was unbelievable good luck.

CHAPTER SEVEN

Uncle Vlodko

Aunt America's coming home with them was not the last of the marvels of that day. For, instead of going home on the autobus, Aunt America explained, they would be going in an automobile. The authorities wished to be sure that she arrived safely in the town, they said, so they had requested that she hire an automobile with a chauffeur who would conduct her there. She would be allowed to return to Kiev on the autobus.

"The automobile will be here soon," Aunt Lydia said. "My only regret is that Lesya will not have seen very much of Kiev on her first visit here. But perhaps I can make it up to her somehow."

Lesya was surprised and even pleased that her aunt had thought of her. She watched her pack a little overnight bag with the things she would need for her stay with them. The foreignness of the things was so intriguing that for the time Lesya almost forgot her wounded feelings. On top, in a little box of their own, her aunt placed some of the things from the bathroom. At last, she snapped shut the lid.

Downstairs, in front of the hotel, a long black limousine, like those officials rode in, waited at the curb. Elena was so impressed that for once even she was silent.

The chauffeur, grand in black uniform and cap, stepped out of the machine. With a grave smile on his broad Russian face, he opened the door for them. First Mama and then Aunt Lydia seated themselves on the back seat; Lesya, her book under her arm, and Elena, with her doll, sat between them. Father and Uncle Vlodko sat facing them on little seats that pulled down.

The chauffeur got into the driver's seat and slammed the door. In a moment they were off. They drove along a steep street that took them down off the bluff to the river's edge, across a bridge, and out into the country. It was a different road from the one they had traveled in the autobus that morning.

No one spoke. Aunt Lydia had the hint of a smile on her face, as if she still could not believe her good fortune. Lesya's thoughts flew ahead. What would people at home think when they saw the black, official limousine drive into town? Lesya already saw the astonishment of everyone when they learned that a visitor from beyond the frontier was among them, right in the town. Such a thing had not happened for more than a generation.

The miles slipped by quickly, and with every mile Lesya's excitement grew. Only now and then, whenever she happened to glance at Elena's doll, did her feeling of elation vanish, and then but for a moment.

Now they were approaching a village. The road was muddy and there were still mounds of snow heaped here and there beside it.

They came to a halt. The chauffeur got out and walked down the road ahead. In front of the village commissary three or four men stood watching him with expressionless faces.

"I wonder what is the matter?" Mama said, craning her neck.

"The road seems to be impassable," Uncle Vlodko said.

Lesya rose halfway from her seat and looked out. The chauffeur stood looking at deep ruts in the road, pushed something with the toe of his boot, and then took off his cap and scratched his head.

When he came back into the automobile, Aunt Lydia said, "Surely you will not try to drive through that?"

"I think it's possible," the chauffeur replied.

Slowly they moved forward into the deep ruts. Then Lesya could feel the wheels moving, but the automobile did not budge. She caught herself leaning tensely forward, as if by doing that she could help the automobile along. She relaxed and sat back. Glancing at Aunt Lydia, she saw a little worried frown playing across her brow.

Now the chauffeur caused the automobile to move backward. Slowly it inched out of the ruts and back onto drier ground. Again the

69

chauffeur got out of the automobile, and this time Father and Uncle Vlodko followed him.

The chauffeur shouted something to the group of men watching them from in front of the commissary. One of the men went inside and in a moment came out with a shovel. He walked over and handed it to the chauffeur. The chauffeur then handed it to Uncle Vlodko, who readily took it and, with the chauffeur standing over him supervising, began to fill the ruts with mud.

"Apparently they think they can smooth the road," Mama remarked.

Aunt Lydia suddenly opened the car door. "This won't do!" she exclaimed, jumping out.

Impelled by her sudden action, Lesya got out, too, and tagged along as her aunt hurried toward the group of men. Aunt Lydia walked up to Uncle Vlodko, gently took the shovel from his grasp, and walked to the chauffeur. Smiling, she held the shovel out to him. "If you please," she said, "This man is my guest. Naturally, then, he must be treated as a guest. Is that not true?"

An astonished expression crossed the chauf-

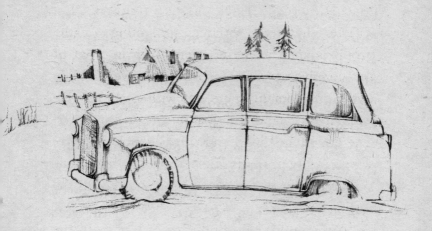

feur's face, as if he had been given a strange, new idea. He took the shovel and stood dangling it uselessly.

Lesya glanced at the men standing about. Suppressed amusement sparkled in their eyes. Uncle Vlodko alone seemed unamused. He stood staring at the mud at his feet.

Father broke the silence. "Why not allow us to proceed on foot?" he asked. "We know the way, and it isn't much farther. It's obvious that the road cannot quickly be smoothed enough for the automobile to pass."

A murmur of agreement rose from the men standing about. The chauffeur stood uncertain for a moment. Then he handed the shovel back to the man who had brought it. "Well, of course, you are right. If you do not mind arriving in the town on foot, you have my permission," he said in a tone of authority.

Aunt Lydia smiled happily. "Thank you!" she cried. "You are very kind!"

Lesya dashed back to the automobile. "Mama!" she cried, "we are walking the rest of the way!"

As they started off down the road, Father carrying Aunt Lydia's little overnight case, Lesya saw that Uncle Vlodko was still embarrassed about something. She frowned, puzzled. It was not like him. He was always so talkative, so sure of himself.

For a while they all walked silently, Mama, Father, and Elena in front, and Aunt Lydia and Uncle Vlodko behind. As Lesya followed along, she studied her aunt. There was something indefinable about the way she walked, as if she were somebody, as if the earth were hers to walk upon.

It reminded Lesya somewhat of the way the Head walked about the town. But not quite. In him there was arrogance, while, like her or not, one could not say there was any arrogance about Aunt Lydia. It was a foreign walk. Lesya wondered, was that the way everyone in America walked?

Aunt Lydia stopped for a moment and as she gazed out over the brown fields rolling away to the horizon her eyes filled with tears. "How beautiful it is!" she said softly to them all. "Only think, I walk my native land once more. Who would have dreamed of such a thing?"

Lesya tried to imagine her aunt's feeling. In a land of wonder like America, did Aunt Lydia sometimes dream, then, of these quite ordinary fields? Lesya looked around her with new eyes.

Suddenly from their right, a loud artificial voice blared out.

"Mercy! What's that?" Aunt Lydia exclaimed, startled out of her mood.

Mama turned around and answered. "The village square must be over there somewhere to our right. And that's the public radio."

"The public radio?" Aunt Lydia repeated.

In a chummy tone, the voice was blaring out something about the plans for the spring planting. Then some jingly-jangly music came blasting out over the serene fields.

"Do you mean to tell me," Aunt Lydia burst out in an indignant voice, "that you must listen to this racket, whether you want to or not?"

Father shrugged his shoulders. "Who listens?" he said curtly.

That was true, Lesya thought. Though every morning as she made her way to school the town radio blared loudly, she could not remember ever really listening to it.

As they started on again, Uncle Vlodko tried to explain. "It's a way for the authorities to reach the people. You see—"

But Aunt Lydia interrupted him. "It's unbearable!" she declared flatly.

That was a new way of looking at it, one that Lesya had not thought of before. She frowned. But surely Aunt Lydia was wrong and Uncle Vlodko, as always, was right?

Aunt Lydia hadn't finished. Carried along by her anger over the radio, she went on, in a low voice, evidently meant only for Uncle

Vlodko, "And why were you so ready with the shovel back there? Don't you realize that that chauffeur was in fact my hireling? Or do you consider him your master?"

Uncle Vlodko hunched his shoulders as if he felt blows upon him. Then he looked at Aunt Lydia. "One has to live," he pleaded.

"To live? And you call that living, to act like—like an ox under a yoke?"

So that's what the episode had meant! But how could Aunt Lydia blame Uncle Vlodko for his behavior? Wasn't it just because he was always willing to do what was expected of him, regardless of what his feelings were, that he had a better job than Father, and his family a better house and better food?

Resentfully Lesya stared at her aunt. What right had she to make such a stir? Why should it matter to her what Uncle Vlodko did and how he lived? She was not being nice, and not behaving at all as a guest should.

Then and there, Lesya decided that there was no longer any doubt about it: she did not and could not like her Aunt Lydia. Let her go back to America where she came from, and leave

75

them in peace!

Unconsciously Lesya allowed her book to slip from under her arm and drop to the ground. At once they were all upon her. Even Uncle Vlodko exclaimed, "Pick it up before it's ruined!"

As Lesya stood looking down at the book, a bitter taste welled into her mouth. Tears of despair filled her eyes at the thought that Aunt America's visit, in which she had put such great hope, was turning out like this. Not only had Aunt America shown that she liked Elena better by giving her the doll, but also—and this was much worse—she plainly showed that she did not approve of Uncle Vlodko.

Lesya had a savage impulse to kick the book out of her sight into the snow mounded beside the road. Instead, she stooped and picked it up.

CHAPTER EIGHT

Grandfather Oak

Although as they at last came walking into town they met no one, Lesya could see the curtains moving in the windows of the houses they passed. She caught glimpses of women hurrying across back yards to neighboring houses, adjusting their kerchiefs as they ran. The whole town was set astir by Aunt Lydia's miraculous appearance among them.

As they approached Uncle Vlodko's house, Aunt Sophia was standing at the gate peering down the road. Word of their arrival had evidently already reached her. Elena broke away from Aunt Lydia's side and ran to her mother. "Mama! Look!" she cried, holding the doll high.

77

Aunt Sophia brushed past her and ran toward them. *"Bozhe!"* she exclaimed. "What miracle has brought you to us?"

The two women embraced for a long moment. As Aunt Lydia at last broke free, she said, "No miracle, Sophia, dear. I asked permission. And received it." She smiled.

Aunt Sophia gazed at her. Then, coming to herself, she assumed her role of hostess. "If you will be so kind," she said, "come into our house."

Now, Lesya thought, Aunt Lydia will see Uncle Vlodko's house. Perhaps when she saw how fine it was, she would change her mind about him. As they stepped into the best room, with its big square table, its great wardrobe, and its double bed piled high with down quilts and enormous square pillows in finely embroidered cases, Lesya kept her eyes on Aunt Lydia.

Her aunt stood for a moment in the middle of the room. As she gazed about, her glance came to rest on the picture of Grandfather that hung on the wall with an embroidered scarf draped over its frame.

78

She walked to the picture and stood gazing at it. Then, turning toward them, she cried, "It does my heart good to see that beautiful Ukrainian embroidery!"

Lesya was astounded. Aunt Lydia, completely ignoring the fine furniture, had chosen the one quite ordinary thing in the room to admire. Every cottage contained such embroidery.

"Then you don't have such things in America?" Aunt Sophia asked.

"Yes, we do," Aunt Lydia replied. "But it's good to see it in its native place."

As Aunt Sophia bustled into the kitchen to prepare refreshments, Lesya put her book on the table and went outdoors. At the front gate, a group of children had gathered. Elena was already holding court among them.

"And why is she so thin?" Mihail asked.

Elena had an answer ready. "That's because she's old. She's my great aunt, you know."

"But her face is not old," Mihail remarked, a frown of doubt on his face. "So I just wonder . . ."

Lesya was gazing at the doll in her cousin's

arms. Elena, noticing, held it out to her. "Want to hold it for a while, Lesya?" she asked.

Lesya's face clouded for an instant. Would it be better to hold it and know what it was like, or not hold it and not know? She couldn't answer her question, but at the same time she couldn't deny herself this chance. Mutely she held out her arms, and Elena laid the doll on them.

Julie now ventured to touch the doll's brunette hair. "Is it real?" she asked.

"Of course!" Elena replied. "And look," she added, tipping the doll's head as it lay on Lesya's arm, "she sleeps!"

"Why!" Maria exclaimed. "She has real lashes! Would you look at that!" She turned to Lesya. "What did your aunt bring you?" she asked.

Before Lesya could answer, Elena said, "A book."

Lesya flared up. "But it's a very beautiful book—and it's more valuable than any old doll!" she cried, handing the doll back.

Now why had she said that? she wondered. She didn't really believe it.

Petro spoke up now. "Did your aunt come all the way from America, all the way across the Atlantic Ocean in an airplane?" His big bony hand zoomed through the air in flight.

"Of course!" Elena said. "But she'll be leaving by train because she wants to see our countryside better."

Petro's hand stopped in midflight. The grownups were coming out into the yard. When Aunt Lydia saw the children, her face brightened. "Well, children," she said, "you have come to see the strange creature from America?"

No one was bold enough to reply.

"But you see," she continued, "I am like you, after all. In fact, I was born here among you; and though I am an American, I am one of you."

"Auntie," Elena spoke up, "they want to know whether you crossed the ocean in an airplane."

Uncle Vlodko stepped forward now and gently said, "Now, children, off with you! It isn't seemly for you to crowd about this way."

Aunt Lydia's eyes smiled regretfully after the retreating children.

Mama said to Lesya, "Come with us, Lesya. Aunt Lydia wishes to tour the town."

There was no escape. Lesya would have to go along. Elena had already grasped Aunt Lydia's hand. Uncle Vlodko and Aunt Sophia and Anya were staying behind.

Because Aunt Lydia said that she wanted especially to visit the old church, they walked down the street toward the edge of town, across a little bridge over the river, and then across fields toward the church.

It rose before them on its hill, its three wooden towers squatting on its roof. A low weather-beaten picket fence surrounded the large church yard. As they drew near, Elena let go of Aunt Lydia's hand and began running ahead. Suddenly she stumbled on a rock and fell headlong.

"Oh!" Lesya cried. "The doll!"

Aunt Lydia glanced sharply at her and then joined the others hurrying to Elena. Elena's face was twisted with pain, but she did not cry. Her knee was badly skinned and blood was oozing out of a long row of scratches on her leg. The doll, Lesya saw, was not broken, but

82

its dress was soiled.

Aunt Lydia, fishing in her large handbag, drew out a clean handkerchief and handed it to Father. "Perhaps this will do to bind the wound," she said.

She took the doll from Elena and brushed the dirt from it. Lesya's hands ached to hold it again, if only for a minute. But Aunt Lydia handed it back to Elena. Father, having brushed the dirt off Elena's leg, was now binding it.

Aunt Lydia turned to Lesya and held out her hand. "Come, Lesya, we'll walk together to the church," she said. "The others can follow."

Lesya's feelings were in a turmoil. Though now she had Aunt Lydia to herself, that could no longer make her happy. For, hadn't she already decided that she did not like this aunt, and even wished her gone? At the same time, just because Aunt Lydia had deliberately chosen to walk alone with her, she wanted to like her aunt. As they climbed the hill, the questions Lesya had been wanting to ask came crowding into her thoughts. But she could not utter a word. She ventured to glance up. Aunt Lydia did not seem embarrassed by the silence.

All the same, Lesya was relieved when they had climbed over the brow of the hill on which the old church, boarded up and abandoned, sat brooding. Its stout, homely timbers were weather-beaten.

The church made Lesya think of Granny Andrushenko, sitting in the sun, old and patient. Granny was so old that she had outlived even some of her grandchildren. Her grey hair was wispy, her face deeply lined, and her lips, for lack of teeth, sunken. But there was something so arrestingly beautiful about her that to look upon her was as refreshing as a drink of cold spring water on a summer day. And when she spoke, rarely as it was, she spoke with such dignity and sharp wisdom that even the Head stood in awe of her.

When Lesya and her aunt reached the great wooden door of the church, they found that through a chink they could peek inside. In the half-light they could see the ancient wall paintings of saints, still flecked with gold, but stained by rain that seeped through the unmended roof. Great cobwebs festooned the altar.

Aunt Lydia was disturbed. "Such a pity," she

said. "Such a great pity to see these works of art uncared for, going to ruin!"

As they walked slowly all around the church, Lesya caught the warm smell of old wood weathering in the sun. When they returned to the front door, she pointed to the tower standing by itself a few steps away. "That is the bell tower, Aunt Lydia," she said. "And look, it's unlocked!"

"Then let's go in!" Aunt Lydia cried.

They climbed up the one high step and through the unlatched door into the tower. It smelled old inside. Before them rose a narrow flight of stairs of rough planks. High among the rafters hung a great iron bell. By silent agreement they started up the stairs, Lesya first. At the top they stood even with the lip of the bell. Aunt Lydia looked up. "Weren't there some more bells here?" she asked.

"Yes, Auntie," Lesya answered. "Father says there were three, but the Germans stole two of them during the war."

A thick rope dangled from the clapper and lay on the boards beneath. Aunt Lydia picked up the end of the rope and snaked it against the bell, and the bell whispered soft and clear. They stood listening to its voice dying away.

Lesya now remembered something. "In the church yard is a very old oak tree that Bohdan Khmelnitzky himself planted three hundred years ago."

Aunt Lydia seated herself on a narrow board that made a bench near the bell. She patted the place beside her. "Come sit with me, Lesya," she said. "Later I want you to show me that tree."

Dutifully Lesya sat down beside her aunt.

"We don't have churches like this in America," Aunt Lydia began. "We have Ukrainian churches, but none as old as this. You are very lucky, Lesya, to be surrounded by the things of your own people—their ancient art and places of history and their songs and stories. Do you like to read?"

Lesya looked up at her aunt. These were new thoughts. "Yes!" she cried. "I always get '5' in reading at school. That's the highest grade."

Aunt Lydia's blue eyes smiled back at her. "I'm glad," she said. "You know, our old Ukrainian tales are better than any toy could

ever be. Toys wear out or one outgrows them.
But the old stories of our people somehow
never wear out! I myself still love to read them,
and I'm a grown woman."

Lesya looked down at her hands. What was
Aunt Lydia trying to say to her? That the book
was more precious than Elena's doll? One part
of her wanted to agree. But the other, stronger,
part of her silently shouted, "But I've never
had a doll!"

Voices came to them then from outdoors.
"What could have happened to them?" Mama's
voice said.

Aunt Lydia smiled mischievously at Lesya
and stood up. Lesya followed her down the
stairs. Outdoors where the rest were, Aunt
Lydia said, "We have been exploring the bell
tower, Lesya and I."

"Aha," Father said, "I thought I heard the
bell, but it was so soft I wasn't sure."

"Lesya is going to show me the oak tree that
Bohdan Khmelnitzky planted," Aunt Lydia
announced.

Though the church yard was very large,
Bohdan's oak dominated one side of it. Lesya

stretched her arms against its trunk and Elena joined her. Even so, their arms failed to reach all the way around the great gnarled trunk.

Together they stood under its wide-spreading branches, still bare of leaves, and looked up. To think that this tree had been planted by Bohdan himself! No matter that this was more legend than fact.

Lesya felt herself sheltered by those fatherly branches. "Grandfather Oak," she said aloud.

CHAPTER NINE

At Dusk

When, late in the afternoon, they returned to Uncle Vlodko's house, Anastasia was waiting for them there. She stood unsmiling as she was introduced to Aunt Lydia.

"Ah, yes," Aunt Lydia said, kissing her on both cheeks, "our families have always been good friends."

Anastasia's face brightened. "Your mother and my grandmother went to school together," she said.

Father spoke up. "For that matter, they went to each other's weddings!"

Aunt Lydia laughed delightedly. Anastasia hesitated, as if she were making up her mind about something. Then she spoke. "Lydia! I have come to beg a great favor of you!"

Aunt Lydia sat down and looked questioningly at her.

"We have a new son, perhaps you have heard," Anastasia went on. "He has not yet been christened. And we have been thinking, my husband and I—" Anastasia was finding it difficult to go on.

Aunt Lydia helped her. "You have been thinking that you would like me to be his godmother? Is that it?" she asked softly.

Relief smoothed Anastasia's face. "Yes," she said. "You know, I have a sister in America, and if it were possible I should like her to be our son's godmother. In her stead, we ask you."

"That is a great honor and a big responsibility," Aunt Lydia said gravely. She smiled. "And I am happy to accept. Whom have you chosen for godfather?"

Anastasia hesitated and then turned toward Uncle Vlodko. "We have not asked him yet. We would like to have Vlodko for the godfather."

Uncle Vlodko reddened with embarrassment

and a pained expression distorted his round face. "I know as well as the next that it isn't seemly to decline such a request. But you all know," he said, appealing to everyone in the room with his arms outspread helplessly, "that if I should appear in church, I would lose my job the next day!"

There was a silence.

Then Father spoke. "He has a better house than most of us, and better food, and better clothes." Father flapped his arms comically. "Now if only the poor devil had wings!"

Aunt Lydia spoke up briskly. "Then whom will you ask?" she said to Anastasia. "Why not Roman?"

And so it was arranged. But Mama, explaining that she was unwilling to have Aunt Lydia go to someone else's house, insisted that the traditional celebration after the christening be held at their house.

As soon as Anastasia left, two or three other neighbors arrived, anxious for a glimpse of the visitor from America. Elena, who had lingered outdoors for a while, now sat beside Aunt Lydia. But Lesya felt she had to get out of the house and away from all the people.

She stepped outside, glanced about, and then started toward the gate. As she drew near it, in the gathering dusk she saw that something was lying on the bench against the fence. When she came near enough to see what it was, she caught her breath.

It was the doll.

Unbelieving, she reached out and touched it. Its eyes, fringed by the lovely lashes, were

closed. How could Elena have left the doll carelessly like this, where any passerby might see it
and perhaps take it?

She looked all around. No one was in sight.
Good. She could play with the doll for a bit
before she carried it into the house. She picked
it up and cradled it in her arms.

At that moment, voices from the house grew
louder. Someone was opening the door and coming out.

Lesya turned, burst through the gate, and
ran down the empty road as hard as she could
run. She looked back and when she saw that
she was out of sight of the house, she slowed
to a walk.

In her arms she still carried the doll. She
would have to go back and return it to Elena.
But behind her now, two figures followed. They
would see that she had the doll. She couldn't
go back! Not now.

She began to run again, ahead toward home.
When she reached the little wooden bridge, as
if she had planned it all along, she scrambled
down to the river's edge and ran along the bank
until she reached the stone foundation.

Breathlessly, as if she were being hotly pursued, she climbed up the stones and shoved the doll into the niche above her. Then she dropped back to the river bank and, panting, stood watching the darkening water flow by.

She listened. No one was coming. In a moment she climbed up the bank, ran lightly across the bridge, and raced home.

CHAPTER TEN

An Important Discovery

The cottage was dark. When Lesya tried the door, she found it locked. She ran around the side of the house and, out of breath, flung herself on the bench against the back of the house.

From somewhere across the fields a cow gave a long, low moo. Lesya giggled. She felt so light-hearted and giddy that she wanted to dance and shout with glee! She had taken the doll and she was glad.

Voices were drawing near the house. She listened. They were coming! And in another moment they were in the house. Mama's voice came floating out to her through the open kitchen window. "Come in! Come in, Aunt

Lydia! Ach! Who would have thought we would be having such a beloved guest in our house!"

Lesya sat up tensely.

Now Father's voice reached her. "I wonder what has happened to our Lesya?"

Tears unexpectedly came into Lesya's eyes at the affectionate way Father spoke of her in her absence. What would he think about the doll? "But I don't care!" Lesya whispered to herself. She drew in her breath and held it, shocked at her new boldness.

The back door opened and Father came out. As he walked toward the woodpile, he saw her. "Why, Lesya, what are you doing out here, all by yourself in the dusk?"

"I was waiting," Lesya managed to say.

"Wait no longer," he said cheerfully, piling kindling on his arm. "Go inside. Aunt Lydia has come home with us!"

Obediently Lesya stood up and walked slowly into the house. The moment she came into the kitchen, Anya came running to her, flung her arms about her, and cried gaily, "Elena has lost her doll!"

Mama was busy putting wood into the stove.
"Yes, poor thing, she is inconsolable. I can't
believe anyone would have taken it. She has
simply misplaced it, and it will turn up. Lesya,
dear, set the table for supper."

As Lesya went to the cupboard, it seemed
that Aunt Lydia was watching her with a
searching look. But it didn't matter! Aunt
Lydia should never have given the doll to
Elena!

Nothing else mattered.

When she carried the dishes to the kitchen
table, she saw that they had brought her book
from Uncle Vlodko's house. She put down the
plates, picked up the book, went into the best
room, and thrust it on the top shelf of the wardrobe, as far back as she could reach. She could
not bear the sight of it.

After supper that night, Father pushed back
his plate and began to talk of his prison experiences. "First they sent us to a labor camp in
Siberia. For months at a time, Auntie, the cold
there hovers at 40 to 50 degrees below zero,
and we worked outdoors. My poor wife—" His
voice grew uncertain. He stopped and looked

down at his hands.

In a moment he looked up and began in a new voice. "Then we were sent to the coal mines of the Donbas. It's a miracle that we are back. Many have not returned. And they never will."

Lesya had never before heard her father tell so much of his experiences and those of Mama while they were imprisoned. In spite of the bitter things he was speaking of, she saw that the look in his blue eyes was gentle, and his wide mouth remained kind.

Lesya glanced at Aunt Lydia, who was listening gravely to every word. On her aunt's face there was not even a shadow of disapproval. On the contrary, it seemed to Lesya that Aunt America was gazing at him with respect.

As Father talked, for some reason Lesya thought of the doll. She had not really meant to take it, she now told herself. But another voice inside her said, "Yes, you did, Lesya. You meant to take the doll all along. You want it!"

Yes, of course she wanted it.

Father was speaking quietly now of how the militia had questioned many in town and searched their cottages again and again in an effort to find some evidence that they, too, were helping the freedom fighters. "Even Vlodko was examined and cross-examined and re-examined," Father ended with a rueful laugh.

"I feel so sorry for Vlodko, I could weep," Aunt Lydia said. "He is a good man. But he is weak. Even under tyranny there is a right way and a wrong way to live."

Lesya stared at her aunt. Uncle Vlodko weak?

Aunt Lydia paused thoughtfully. Then she said, "But perhaps it is not for me to say such a thing. Which of us can say whether under oppression he would always act with courage? I live in freedom, and I cannot say. In America," she went on, "we believe this: every freedom must be continually used or it will wither away. Here, it seems to me, where there is so little, the most important thing is for everyone to use to the full even the smallest freedom granted them. And at the same time never for a moment stop pressing for more—and more!"

Mama's eyes softened as she gazed at Aunt Lydia. "Tell us about America, Auntie, for we shall never see it!"

Now was Lesya's chance to ask the reason for Aunt Lydia's thinness and the other things she had been wondering about. But she did not want to call attention to herself. For one thing, Mama might suddenly notice how far past her bedtime it was and send her off. Anya had long ago been put to bed and was fast asleep.

Aunt Lydia described her house and the city she lived in. Yet, it was not easy to capture America from what she was telling them. It was all too strange.

Aunt Lydia delved into her handbag finally and brought out pictures of her family. When Mama handed the pictures to Lesya, she looked at them for a long time, trying to imagine from the faces what America was like. And to think that they were her own family, and lived in that country so strange, so far away that it seemed only a fable!

At last Mama poured a final cup of tea for them. There was not only milk, but also sugar lumps that Aunt Lydia had brought from the hotel in Kiev. As they sipped their nightcap of tea, Aunt Lydia remarked that she was sorry that Lesya had seen so little of Kiev on her first visit there. But perhaps, she suggested, Mama or Father would take her again. "It will be my treat," she said.

She drew a ruble note from her pocketbook and held it out to Lesya. Lesya hesitated to take it. A feeling of shame flooded through her, and she was sure that it was plain on her face. Father became annoyed at what he thought was her shyness. "Lesya," he prompted.

Lesya took the money gingerly, as if it would burn her fingers. "Thank you, Auntie," she whispered.

As she went into the other room to hide the note in the pocket of her coat, hanging in the wardrobe, she was startled to see that Aunt Lydia had given her five rubles. Aunt Lydia had no idea of their money. Why, that was enough for several trips to Kiev!

Lesya was just closing the door of the wardrobe when she realized that in the other room they were talking about her. She listened.

"The hardest part of all, Auntie," Father was saying, "was having to leave our Lesya to an unknown fate. What anguish we suffered over this! We could only hope that Vlodko would take pity on our little daughter."

"Thank God Sophia had it in her heart to take her to them," Mama said. "And, for the matter of that, Vlodko, too. They were both kind to our child."

Lesya stood in a trance.

For a mindless, numb moment she stood there. And there came back to her, as if it were all happening over again, the terror of being left behind, of being forsaken by her own parents. Lesya's eyes burned again with the tears she had not been able to weep then and would not weep now.

The parting, then, had been as terrible for her mother and father as it had been for her. They had been anxious about her. Though she had often thought of that time, this blazing truth had never come to Lesya. But now she had heard it, from the lips of her own father.

Lesya stood motionless, unwilling to move, marveling over what pure happiness felt like.

Someone came in. It was Mama.

Lesya looked at her, ready to rush into her arms at the slightest glance from her. But her mother did not notice. Instead, she began to bustle about fixing a bed for Aunt Lydia on the divan. Slowly Lesya closed the door of the wardrobe and began to help her.

CHAPTER ELEVEN

The Christening Party

When Lesya opened her eyes the next morning, for a moment she had to think where she was. A murmur of voices came from the kitchen and one of them was strange. Then she sat up with a jerk. Aunt America! Aunt America was in their house and Lesya was wasting her time in bed. Even Anya, she saw, was no longer beside her.

Then Lesya sank back on her pillow and stared at the ceiling. She had taken Elena's doll. As she lay there, remembering, she could hardly believe that she had done this. The triumph she had felt over having taken the doll had utterly vanished.

She sat up again and slowly got out of bed. As soon as she was dressed, she would have to go and retrieve the doll and return it to Elena. Half listening to the murmur of talk in the kitchen, punctuated by Anya's bright voice, Lesya reached for her petticoat. As she moved quietly about she savored the delicious presence of her aunt from America here in this very house with them.

Lesya did not have to be told why, though there was room for an overnight guest at Uncle Vlodko's, Aunt Lydia had spent the night with them instead. Everyone wanted to spare Uncle Vlodko the burden of Aunt Lydia's presence in his house. Instinctively Lesya knew that though Aunt Lydia was Uncle Vlodko's own aunt, in his position it was not well for him to be too intimate with this stranger from America. Father and Mama felt no such constraint.

As Lesya pulled her sweater over her head, she had a curious thought: Father and Mama were really more free than Uncle Vlodko. Why, he could not even be godfather to Anastasia's baby!

As Lesya stepped into the kitchen and saw

her father, happiness on his face, sitting at the table opposite Aunt Lydia, she had the impulse to go to him and kiss him good morning. But she hesitated. How could she? She wasn't worthy! Not until she had returned the doll would she be worthy.

Having exchanged morning greetings, Lesya quietly slipped onto the bench beside Aunt Lydia. Anya was sitting on Aunt Lydia's lap, sucking one of the sugar lumps. Though Mama was already busy with preparations for the christening party, she had Lesya's breakfast ready. Lesya sipped the hot, sweetened tea and ate a bit of the bread.

The moment she finished eating, Lesya decided, she would see to the doll. Then she would be free to enjoy the day.

Mama brought out of the storage place one of the precious sausages she had made for the coming Easter and began to slice it. Just as Father and Aunt Lydia were leaving for Anastasia's house, from where they would carry the infant to church to be christened, some of Anastasia's neighbor women came. One brought two platters of little sweet cakes. Others came with bowls of pirohi filled with potato, cabbage, and even bits of meat.

Soon the cottage was alive with chatter and laughter and even snatches of singing from the women. Never before in Lesya's memory had there been a party in their house. She had sometimes listened to grownups remind each other of weddings and christenings that had lasted several days. But that was in olden times.

Now, Lesya decided, was the time for her to slip out, for in the happy hubbub she would not be missed. But just at that moment, Mama, her face flushed with unusual gaiety, discovered that Anya had found one of the platters of little cakes on the table in the best room. "Lesya!" she cried. "Go outdoors, and take Anya with you."

Lesya caught her little sister by the hand. Could she leave her alone in the yard, perhaps, while she dashed to the bridge? But when she stepped outdoors, she realized that some of her playmates had gotten wind of the coming festivities and were hanging about the gate. "Hey! Lesya! Come and play with us!" they called as soon as they saw her.

"Did you hear," someone called out, "that Elena's doll is missing?"

"Poor Elena! Who do you suppose could have done such a thing?" Julie said.

Lesya cringed inside. She would have to return the doll immediately. "Maria," she said, "mind my little sister for a bit, will you? I'll be back soon."

"Why? Where are you going?"

"I'm going to—I'm just—I want to go for a little walk," Lesya finished lamely.

With that, she already knew what was coming.

"Then let me go with you!" Maria cried.

"Me, too!" Julie put in.

"We'll all go!" Mihail shouted.

Lesya stood at the gate, thwarted. How could they be so contrary? When you wanted them about, where were they? And when you didn't —well, she would have to put off returning the doll for a bit.

"I'll tell you what," she said, "instead, I'll bring out my book and we can all look at it."

"Bring it, then!" Petro said. "Who cares about walking?"

Lesya ran into the cottage and came back with the book. They clustered around as she sat on the bench. First they admired the picture of the Daughter of the Sun on the cover. "I once saw such a book as this on a bookstall in Kiev," Petro announced.

Lesya herself turned the pages. The *ohs* and *ahs* that came with each new page were satisfying. Never before had Lesya owned anything that others admired.

"Oh," Julie cried excitedly, "there's the story of Sir Cat. My mother has told me that selfsame story hundreds of times!"

"Wait! Not so fast!" Petro exclaimed, trying to turn back a page.

"Not with your grubby fingers!" Maria cried, as if the book belonged to all of them. "Do you want to spoil it?"

Petro hastily rubbed his hands on his pants and gently turned back the page.

They were so absorbed in the book that they did not see the grownups approaching with the newly christened infant until they had reached the gate and were passing through. Then the children turned from the book and watched.

Aunt America, followed by the others, was carrying the infant on a long pillow covered with a bit of lace. She smiled. "Do you want to see my godson?" she asked them.

Seating herself on the bench, she lifted the lace off the child's face. "His name is Andriy," she said.

Andriy was fast asleep. When he grew up enough to understand, his mother would tell him about his American godmother, and he would not be able to realize such a thing to himself. Now in his sleep he smacked his lips.

"Did he cry while he was being christened?" Lesya wanted to know. "That would mean he is going to be a good singer."

Aunt America laughed and stood up. "No," she said, "he was as quiet as a little mouse!"

When Aunt America and the rest had gone indoors, Lesya closed her book. Followed by some of her girl friends, she too went inside.

In the best room, the grownups stood around the table, spread festively, to drink a toast, first to the new child, then to his godparents and parents. Mama, as the hostess, had to see to it that the guests' glasses were filled, that the

III

platters of food were not empty. She did not
forget to pass a platter of cakes among Lesya's
friends. Occasionally, she proposed a toast of
her own, and then everyone stood and in honor
of the person toasted sang a verse of the song,
"Many Years."

The infant lay sleeping on the bed, unmindful
of the celebration in his honor. Anya had

climbed onto Father's lap and sat contentedly
chewing on a piece of sausage. Father began
to tell of a funny escapade of his youth.

As Lesya listened, she looked around at the
others. They were all listening to her father with
friendly eyes, and even with a certain respect,
as if he were somebody. She could not remember anyone ever looking at Uncle Vlodko in

quite that way. Father's story reminded his listeners of others and an endless round of anecdotes began.

Aunt America, Lesya noticed, did not talk much. She sat, her eyes shining, and listened as if she were learning by heart everything that was said and done.

In the midst of the story-telling, Uncle Vlodko, Aunt Sophia, and Elena came. Room was somehow made for them at the table. Several asked after the missing doll, as if it were a lost child. "Poor Elena!" they said.

As Lesya stood watching, she realized she could not return the doll directly to her cousin. If she did that, she would have to confess that she had taken it. Then everyone would talk endlessly about it. She could hear them now: "To think that Elena's own cousin, her own flesh and blood, did such a monstrous thing against her! Ach, tell me, whom can you trust nowadays?"

Yet, Lesya could not freely enjoy the festivities until she had returned the doll. Could she say that she had merely kept it safe for Elena, who had carelessly left it outdoors on the bench? No! That was a lie, and everyone would know it. Better just to take it back to the bench where she had found it, and let people think what they would. That was the only way she could free herself of the trouble she had gotten herself into.

Quietly, while Maria wasn't looking, Lesya slipped outdoors. She went to the gate and looked up and down the road. It was empty. Opening the gate, she ran down the road toward the bridge.

When she reached it, she stopped and listened. Voices were coming from below. She stepped over to the railing and looked down. What did she see but Mihail and Petro, sitting on the bank, fishing. The river was she knew not how many miles long, but they had to choose this precise spot to be. She ignored the fact that this was where they usually fished.

"Will you be long?" she found herself foolishly calling down to them.

"Be quiet!" Mihail called back. "You'll scare off the fish!"

Lesya hung about, not knowing what to do now. At last, seeing there was no use waiting for the boys to leave, she started for home again. It had not been a good plan anyway, she told herself as she scuffed thoughtfully along. Supposing she had managed to get the doll from its hiding place, carry it unseen through town, and put it back on the bench? That would not have been a safe thing to do, for someone might then have chanced by and taken it. Then it would have been lost in truth. She would have to wait till dusk.

She stopped in the middle of the road. What if the boys should start climbing about under the bridge, as they often did, and find the doll? Unreasonably Lesya began to hate the doll, as if it were a person, for all the trouble it was causing her. She wished she had never laid eyes on it!

As she neared the house, she saw that Uncle Vlodko, Aunt Sophia, and Elena were walking toward her. They had not stayed long at the party, but that was understandable. Lesya felt that the instant they looked at her face they would know her guilt. She glanced to the side of the road for a place to hide. But there was nowhere to hide, and in any case, they had already seen her.

Aunt Sophia spoke. "What's the matter, Lesya? Tired of the festivities?"

"I was—I was just taking a walk," Lesya managed to reply.

"Taking a walk!" Elena cried, as if she had never heard of anything so foolish.

"I must hurry home now," Lesya said, suddenly breaking into a run.

She knew they were all looking at her with curiosity, and perhaps with suspicion, too.

She pushed through the gate and flung herself on the bench, out of breath. From the cottage came sounds of singing, and someone was playing a bandura. It must be Antin, for he was one of the few who owned a bandura and knew how to play it expertly. The music calmed her a little, and soon she felt able to go inside.

They were still sitting around the table. But some people had gone and others had come in their places. Maria, too, had gone. Lesya looked at her father. He was laughing at something someone had just said. Anya still sat on his lap, but now she was leaning against his chest asleep. What would Father say if he knew that she, Lesya, was the thief who had stolen the doll?

Suddenly Lesya wanted to cry. She wanted to hide her face on Father's shoulder and weep.

Noticing Lesya, Aunt Lydia stretched out her arm and drew her close. Lesya stood there in despair. Would Aunt Lydia have done that if she had known what a shameful thing she had done? Much as she now wanted to, Lesya could not enjoy her aunt's affection.

Someone pushed a chair in place for Lesya and she sat down next to her aunt. During a lull in the singing, Antin, on the other side of Aunt Lydia, said as he softly fingered the strings of his instrument, "Lydia, do you know, I have a sister in America. She lives in Detroit."

Aunt Lydia nodded.

"Would you be willing," he went on, "to take a letter to her? I have already written it. There is nothing of great importance in it, but perhaps you could—" He broke off and started again. "We are not able, you know, to write as we wish."

"Yes, yes, I understand," Aunt Lydia said.

118

"When I send her the letter, I myself will also write that I saw you with my own eyes and that—"

Antin did not wait for her to finish. "Tell her," he said, "how we are forced to live, how we—" He broke off and could not go on.

Aunt Lydia looked at his bowed head with tears in her eyes. "Never fear," she said quietly. "I will know what to write."

Antin drew the letter out of his jacket pocket and handed it to Aunt Lydia. "May the Lord bless you!" he said.

Aunt Lydia carefully put the letter into her dress pocket. Soon after, Antin rose to go. He embraced Aunt Lydia, kissed her on both cheeks, and too full for words, made his way out of the cottage.

One by one, several others came to sit beside Aunt Lydia during the afternoon and, in the midst of the talk and laughter, privately gave her letters of greeting to take to dear ones in America. They asked that in addition she convey messages they were unable to write. Aunt Lydia accepted each letter and promised to deliver the messages when she arrived home.

119

At last, toward dusk, Anastasia began to bundle up the still-sleeping infant. Her husband, seeing that she was preparing to leave, stood up and said with a wink, "Well, brothers mine, we must not prolong our entertainment or our beloved Head will get the silly notion that we are plotting some kind of mischief here."

Soon after the final guest had departed, Aunt Lydia began to pack her overnight case. It was almost time for her to leave them. As Lesya watched her aunt, panic came over her. The parting would be forever. When the time came to say farewell, each had to be at peace with himself and with the other. Without fail, therefore, Lesya had to tell her aunt about the doll. Otherwise, there would always be that ugly deceit between them.

For the moment, only Anya was in the room with them. She was sitting on the floor playing with the clasp on Aunt Lydia's handbag. Lesya sighed. "Auntie?" she began.

Her aunt looked up at her expectantly. "Yes, Lesya, dear?"

Lesya found herself totally without courage. "Write to us," she said.

Her aunt went back to her packing. "Yes, of course, my darling. I will write a letter just for you. And you must answer. Will you do that?"

As it turned out, the worst possible thing happened. At the last moment, when Aunt Lydia wordlessly held her tight in her arms, and Lesya could have whispered in her ear, even then she did not have the courage to speak. She let her aunt go without a word.

The day of the christening, Lesya decided, was a black day in her life.

CHAPTER TWELVE

The Letters

The night that Aunt America left them, Lesya lay in bed so tired that she could no longer feel anything. But, tired as she was, her thoughts would not let her sleep. They wandered aimlessly through her mind like ghosts lost on a great empty plain veiled in fog, appearing out of the mist and disappearing into it.

One of her thoughts was so real that she sat up in bed and looked over at the divan where Aunt Lydia had slept. No one was there. She sank back on her pillow.

Her thoughts were in Kiev now, in the little park with the playground. She tried again to feel the rhythm and freedom of swinging high into the air. But she was too tired now.

In the dark, Lesya frowned. There was something else there that she must remember. But what was it? Whatever it was, it was lost in the mist and would not come out. "Well, it doesn't matter," Lesya whispered aloud.

Now the doll came wandering into her thoughts. She had not yet returned it. Wearily, she began to wonder for what reason Aunt Lydia had given her the book and Elena the doll. What if it had been the other way around? No, that would not have been right. Elena would never have been pleased with the book. She simply wasn't the sort. Whereas, if only there had been no doll, Lesya would have been overjoyed with the book.

Aunt Lydia had somehow sensed this difference between her and Elena. That was why, then, she had given her the book.

As for the hateful doll, she hoped that it still lay hidden under the bridge. She took a long, deep breath. Tomorrow, without fail, she must restore the doll to Elena. She felt no need to tell Elena of her deed. She had done it against Aunt Lydia and, in some mysterious way,

123

against her father, too. They were the ones she must tell.

In the next room, Father stirred and muttered something in his sleep. Lesya, too, fell asleep at last.

She had been asleep for hours, when suddenly she was awake again, staring wide-eyed into the dark. She sat up. The letters! The memory that had escaped her before was clear in her mind now. Aunt Lydia had packed the six letters that had been given her into her suitcase. Lesya had watched her do it.

And in the park—had it really been only the day before yesterday?—the two men at the swings had talked of someone who had been caught at the border with uncensored letters.

Lesya's heart began to pound.

Just from the way Aunt Lydia had slipped those letters into her suitcase, Lesya knew that her aunt did not realize the danger of it. If Father had seen her do it, Lesya was sure he would have warned her to hide them. Just because Aunt Lydia was not used to the way they had to live, she did not realize the need to be careful.

124

Lesya dropped back on her pillow. But what could she do? After all, she was not a grownup. Perhaps this was not really her concern. Hadn't she often heard Uncle Vlodko say, "Don't concern yourself with matters that are none of your business. Mind your own affairs, and all will be well"?

Lesya tried to go back to sleep. But she could not even close her eyes. She watched the dawn slowly light the room. Today, Aunt Lydia was getting on the train that would take her to the border and out of the country. At the border, they would open her suitcase and find the letters and—Lesya did not want to imagine the rest.

But she could not stop her thoughts. They would question Aunt Lydia severely, but in the end, probably, they would have to let her go. They would take the letters from her, of course.

And then—Lesya was struck with a new thought. Why then, they would begin to question those who had written the letters. There was Antin and Anastasia and Petro's father. . . . They might even question Father and Mama again because they, unlike Uncle Vlodko, had had the courage to have Aunt Lydia, and the

people who had come to see her, in their house.
There would be no end to the trouble.

Lesya sat up and thrust one foot out of bed.
Should she wake Father and tell him? No. She
would not wake him. She would take the early
autobus to Kiev and go herself. She had things
to say to her aunt personally because she had
personally done something against her.

Lesya crept out of bed and began to dress by
the dawning light. She held her breath as Anya
stirred. Her little sister smacked her lips, flipped
over, and slept.

Lesya opened the wardrobe door ever so carefully, praying that it wouldn't squeak, and took
out the coat into whose pocket she had put the
money Aunt Lydia had given her. As she put
it on, she smiled to herself. Neither of them had
dreamed that she would be making that journey
to Kiev so soon.

Lesya stood in the middle of the room.
Should she write a note to Father and Mama,
tell them where she was going? No. She would
have to hunt up paper and pencil and that, perhaps, would awaken everybody. Besides, she
knew that Father would not be angry with her

for what she was doing.

Now came the hardest part. She had to steal out of the house without waking her parents. She took a deep breath, held it, and tiptoed across the room to the doorway. There she stood still a moment, took another deep breath, and started across the kitchen for the door. Luckily, Father was now snoring loudly so that if a floor board creaked, it would not be heard. Lesya smiled to herself. Sometimes Father snored like a bear, and it used to scare her.

At the door now, ever so gently, she pressed down the latch. At that moment Father suddenly broke off snoring. Her heart pounding, Lesya stook quite still. If her father should open his eyes, he would see her!

Lesya waited for whatever might come. After a moment Father began to snore again. Swiftly she swung the door open, let herself out, and softly shut it again.

Outdoors, she let out a long breath. Low in the sky, the moon hung over the orchard across the road. She listened. In the whole town there wasn't a sound. She hurried through the gate, turned to the right, and broke into a run.

When she got to the bridge she slowed to a walk, then stopped. Shouldn't she settle the matter of the doll right now? No one would see her, and when Aunt Sophia opened her door first thing this morning, she would find the doll on the door step.

Lesya ran across the bridge on tiptoe, so as not to make any sound on the wooden planks, and scrambled down the steep bank to the river. Under the bridge, she climbed up on its stone foundation. Luckily, even in the darkness, she knew every handhold and foothold. When she reached the place, she stretched her hand to the ledge above and blindly searched.

For an instant, she was scared. Her hand found nothing. Could Petro or Mihail have found the doll and made off with it?

She tried again. This time her fingers touched something soft. Just barely managing to grasp it, she pulled down the doll. Holding it tightly, she climbed safely down to the water's edge.

Back on the road, she stood and looked at the doll. It gazed innocently back at her from beneath its lashes.

Now she flew like the wind toward Uncle

Vlodko's. When she got there, she saw that there was a light on in the house. Evidently someone was already up. Carefully she laid the doll on the doorstep and, without a backward glance, ran lightly toward the square in the middle of town.

It was just six as she reached the cobbled square, for at that moment the radio blasted out, shattering the lovely dawn stillness.

When she climbed into the autobus standing on the square, she saw that every seat was already taken. Talk stopped and heads turned as she made her way down the aisle. Only as short a time ago as yesterday, she would have wanted to run away from so much attention. Now, for some reason, she rather enjoyed it as she continued down the aisle to the front of the bus.

Maria's mother sat on the long seat at the front. As she moved over to make room for Lesya, she asked, "And where are you off to, child?"

Before Lesya could answer, Mihail's father spoke up. "It's evident she cannot bear to let go of her auntie from America. Isn't it true, Lesya?"

Lesya nodded. "I'm going to Kiev to see Auntie Lydia off!" she said.

"And school can wait. Is that it?" Mihail's father added.

"Ach! Who can blame the child?" Maria's mother said.

Soft exclamations came from up and down the bus. Soon they started off. Though the sun had not yet risen, it was broad daylight.

CHAPTER THIRTEEN

An Urgent Matter

"Mind you don't get lost!" several voices called as Lesya alighted from the autobus in Kiev and started across the wide street in the direction of Aunt Lydia's hotel. She was sure she knew the way. Yes, there was the big department store on the corner.

Though it was still rather early in the morning, the sidewalks were crowded with people. Some of them looked curiously at her, as if they knew she did not belong. Lesya tried to walk along the way Aunt Lydia did. But inside, she was frightened.

It was a long walk to the hotel, she knew that. She kept expecting to come to the place where the chessboard had been, with the crowd standing in front of it. But after a while, when she still had not come to it, she began to feel that she had been walking longer than she should have.

She stopped and looked around. Suddenly, nothing looked familiar. But she decided to walk a little farther in the direction she had been going. If only she would come to one familiar spot, she knew she could find her way.

But everything continued to look strange, and she began to feel panicky. If she took too long to find the hotel, her aunt would be gone. She would ride toward the border unaware of the danger that might be awaiting her there. Further than that, Lesya did not want to think. She had to find Aunt Lydia!

Suddenly, against the sky, Lesya caught a glimpse of a golden cupola. St. Sophia! She hurried toward it.

When she arrived opposite it, to her right she saw the little green place with the statue of Bohdan Khmelnitzky. And there, walking up and down, was the photographer who had taken their picture.

Lesya picked her way across the broad street toward the statue. At first, the photographer looked at her as if he had never seen her before.

"Don't you remember me?" she asked anxiously. "I was here the day before yesterday with my aunt."

"Aha!" the man smiled. "The lady from America! But I have already taken the pictures to her, little girl." He cocked his head and asked, "And shouldn't you be on your way to school?"

"But I wish to see my auntie first," Lesya said.

"And you have lost your way. Is that it? Well, it isn't far. You go straight down this street, past St. Sophia, past the Golden Gates, and then turn left. The hotel is only a few steps beyond the corner. But you'd better hurry! When I brought your aunt the photographs this morning, she was already packing."

Lesya thanked the man and hurried off. When she heard the welcome sound of the ravens that nested near the Golden Gates, she felt better. Five minutes later she stood in front of the hotel.

133

Now came the hardest part of all. For the first time that morning, Lesya faltered. What if the woman did not allow her to see Aunt Lydia? She recalled the questioning Uncle Vlodko had had to undergo before they were allowed to go down the corridor. Lesya wasn't sure that before such questioning she would not give up and flee for home.

But what had to be done, had to be done. She pushed through the door, crossed the lobby, and walked up the stairs to the second floor. There, at the head of the stairs, sat the woman. Leaning against the wall beside her was a man in a chauffeur's uniform, but not the same man who had driven them two days before. He and the woman were busy talking. What luck! Perhaps, Lesya thought, she could slip past them. She knew the way to Aunt Lydia's room.

Neither of them seemed to notice her as she started down the corridor. But she had gone only a few steps when the woman called after her, "And where do you think you are going, little girl?"

Lesya felt an impulse to run. If she could just reach the safety of her aunt's room, she felt all would be well. Instead, she turned back. Her heart pounded so hard that she thought it would leap right through her chest. She heard a strange, thin little voice say, "I've come to see my aunt." It was her own voice, she realized.

Looking steadily at her without any expression on her face, the woman said, "You wish to see her?"

"Yes, please."

"Shouldn't you be on your way to school— at this time of day? And where are your manners, that you think of bursting in on people without notice?"

Just because this remark was unreasonable, it gave Lesya courage. She remembered Father's way of making a request as if he had a moral right to it. Lesya ignored the question about school. She heard herself saying, "If you please, I wish to see her."

"About some urgent matter?" the woman pursued.

"Yes, urgent," Lesya replied.

The woman glanced at her companion. Instantly Lesya realized her mistake. If the woman knew that the matter was urgent, she might try to find out what it was. "That is," Lesya went on, "I wish to say goodbye to my aunt."

The woman leaned back in her chair. "Only to say goodbye?"

Lesya nodded.

"Your aunt has already gone," the woman now said.

Lesya stood speechless.

"Not half an hour ago, she left for the railroad station," the woman added. "A pity you should have missed her."

Now for the first time, the man spoke. "A pity, indeed," he said, giving Lesya a friendly glance. "It is not every day that one has a guest from America!" He looked at his wristwatch. "The train doesn't leave for half an hour. I'll drive the child over, and she'll have at least fifteen minutes to spare in which to say goodbye."

The woman seemed about to protest.

"I have money," Lesya said quickly.

The man waved his hand. "Ach, money!" he exclaimed. He stretched his arm toward the stairs. "If you please," he said to Lesya.

Quickly she ran down the stairs with the chauffeur. Outside, at the curb, stood a machine. Just as if she were a grownup lady, he opened the door for her and helped her into the seat beside him. As they started off, he said, "I myself put your aunt on the train, so I know which compartment she's in. Never fear! We'll find your auntie!"

His easy, friendly manner calmed Lesya. Here she was in Kiev, riding in a limousine like an official! But now a new worry crept into her thoughts. To do what she had come to do, she would need to be alone with her aunt. If there were others in the compartment, how could she tell her aunt about the letters?

CHAPTER FOURTEEN

The Proud, Free Way

At the crowded railroad station Lesya hurried along beside the chauffeur through the big waiting room and into the train shed. A long train stood on the tracks. Lesya's heart quickened as they hurried along beside it. Presently the chauffeur stopped beside a train door. "Here we are and up you go!" he said, helping her up the steps into the train.

Lesya ran along the corridor. The compartment doors were all open, and she glanced into each as she hurried past. Not one was occupied. But in one of the compartments almost at the end of the corridor, she saw a familiar figure sitting alone.

Aunt Lydia looked up and seeing her standing in the doorway, cried, "Lesya! My dear—!"

She rose and caught Lesya in her arms.

In that instant all of Lesya's new courage melted away as if it had never been. Purely out of relief to be safe with Aunt Lydia at last, she began to sob silently. Aunt Lydia pressed her closer. "There, there, my darling. How happy I am you came!"

The chauffeur appeared in the doorway. "Your niece," he said, "could not bear to let you go without another goodbye."

Aunt Lydia looked at her. "Are you alone, then? And you will be going home on the autobus?"

Lesya wiped her tears on her sleeve and nodded.

Aunt Lydia turned toward the chauffeur. He was leaning against the doorway as if he intended to stay until the train started. "Perhaps you will be willing to wait," she said to him, "and after we've said our goodbyes, drive my niece to the autobus that will take her home." She opened her purse and drew out some money. "This will pay for her fare," she said, handing it to him.

The chauffeur smiled as he took the money. "In that case, I will wait outside, on the platform."

As soon as he was gone, Aunt Lydia drew her down on the seat, and looked searchingly into her face. "Now, Lesya, tell me, is something the matter?"

In whispers, Lesya told what she had overheard in the playground and explained the danger of carrying uncensored letters.

140

Aunt Lydia listened gravely. *"Bozhe!"* she breathed, when Lesya had finished. "What a fool I am! You're quite right, Lesya. I did not realize the danger, and those letters are scattered through my luggage. Everyone who gave me a letter expected me to know how to behave. But you see, Lesya, I am not used to—in America we—" She did not finish.

Instead, she rose, opened the little suitcase lying on the seat opposite, and searched through the luggage inside. One by one, she found the letters, six of them. Just as she snapped the suitcase shut again, a man poked his head in at the doorway. He looked curiously at Lesya, and then said to Aunt Lydia, "The train leaves in ten minutes."

"Thank you, conductor. I shall see that my niece gets off in good time."

The man walked on. Aunt Lydia sat down again and began searching for something in her purse. "There is no need for me to take the letters at all," she said.

Lesya stared at her aunt. She had insisted that she wished to do this great favor for people. Now, in the face of the first difficulty, was she giving up?

"I will copy off the names and addresses so that I'll know whom to write to," Aunt Lydia continued. "And you, Lesya, can take the letters back home and tell them what I have done. Tell them they may depend on me to deliver their messages."

She drew a tiny notebook and pen from her purse and hurriedly began copying the addresses off the envelopes. Lesya's heart pounded with fright. What if someone should come by and see her aunt writing something in a notebook? It did not look well. Aunt America did not know the first thing about being careful! Lesya got up and stood in the doorway of the compartment.

The train gave a sudden lurch. Just at that moment, finished copying, Aunt Lydia gathered up the letters and stuffed them into Lesya's coat pocket. Fortunately, it was large enough so that they didn't make her coat bulge. In addition, she gave Lesya two copies of the pictures taken in the park.

"Lesya," Aunt Lydia said, "you will want to know what happens at the border. I will write to your parents when I arrive home. I will not be able to write clearly, but if I say in my letter, 'Give a special kiss from me to Lesya,' that will mean that at the border they searched my luggage for letters and, thanks to you, found none."

The train lurched again. Lesya was frantic. There was no more time! And she still hadn't told about the doll. Hurriedly, Aunt Lydia hugged her and kissed both her cheeks. Then

143

she drew her out into the corridor and, holding
onto her hand, ran to the end of the car. The
conductor was standing on the platform below,
waiting to fold back the little steps into the
doorway.

Come what may, Lesya had to tell her aunt.
She would not feel right until she did. Just putting the doll back was not enough. Her words
tumbling over each other, Lesya poured out the
story of the doll and of how, that morning, she
had returned it.

Aunt Lydia looked at her with shining eyes.
"Yes, I know, Lesya. And I knew you would
return it! You are a brave girl to tell me about
it." She paused. "You have some of your father's
courage. I am thankful for that," she whispered.

The conductor lifted the little steps and irri-
tably banged them down again. "Enough!
Enough!" he cried.

Aunt Lydia kissed her lightly on both cheeks
again and let her go. She jumped down the steps
and the conductor immediately folded them
back. Then he slammed the door shut.

Lesya stood watching the train slowly rumble
down the tracks, out of the train shed, toward

the horizon, where, somewhere, far beyond lay America. As she felt the quickening rhythm of the wheels clicking against the tracks, her feeling of bereavement grew and grew until a big lump of grief filled her chest. Though letters would go back and forth between them, never again could they exchange a free word with each other. To keep from weeping aloud, Lesya pressed her lips together.

Someone touched her arm. "Come, child," the chauffeur said quietly. "We must all learn to say goodbye, and without lingering." He sighed and smiled at her. "I know! From experience!"

The chauffeur succeeded in driving her to the autobus stop just as one was about to leave. "Cheer up!" he said, as he waved goodbye.

On the autobus were a number of the townspeople, already returning from market. Lesya again sat down beside Maria's mother. "Well, so you've seen your auntie off?"

"Yes, she's gone."

Lesya thrust her hand into her coat pocket and fingered the letters and the two pictures. Aunt Lydia had known about her guilt all along.

And in spite of that, she had loved her. Lesya gave a deep sigh. That was a miracle, she thought.

Only now did Lesya realize that she had neglected to ask the reason for her aunt's thinness. Well, it didn't matter.

Somehow Lesya had a clear glimpse of America from what Aunt Lydia was. She saw it in the animated, pleasant way she talked; in the careful way she listened, even to a child; in the proud, free way she walked.

Now that Lesya was on the way home, she could hardly wait to get there. She felt a sudden, overwhelming yearning to see her father. Just because of Aunt Lydia's visit, in her thoughts Father and Uncle Vlodko had changed places. Father's life was harder, but it was freer, and better because it was right. He lived for others as well as for himself.

Aunt America's visit had already become a dream almost too hard to recapture, when a letter from her finally came. At the end of it she wrote, "And give a special kiss from me to Lesya." Lesya explained to Father and Mama just what that meant.

Weeks after the letter, a package arrived from America. In it was a warm jacket for Father, to replace the cheap, shabby one he had been wearing for as long as Lesya could remember. There was a pretty wool dress for Mama; a sweater, blue as the summer sky, for Lesya; and a snowsuit for Anya that made her look like an adorable little bear cub. And, at the very bottom of the box lay a doll. To its dress was pinned a note, "For Lesya!"

As she held the doll in her arms, the cottage was suddenly too small to hold her feelings. Though the autumn dusk had already fallen, Lesya went to the wardrobe for her coat. She put it on and, carefully carrying the doll, went outdoors.

"Lesya!" Mama called after her, "where are you off to?"

Father's voice quietly said, "Let her go."

Lesya smiled to herself. Father understood.

As if her legs already knew where she was going, her steps took her across the bridge, down the road toward the edge of town, straight across the bare fields to the old church. When she reached the church yard, she stood for a moment and looked at the great oak, its every branch illuminated with snow. She imagined the day Bohdan Khmelnitzky had come galloping to this spot on which she now stood and, probably among a great throng of people, had planted a little oak tree. Very likely, among that throng, mounted and banners flying, had been some of her own forefathers.

Feeling an unusual importance within herself, Lesya turned and made her way to the bell tower. Snow had drifted against its door, but Lesya managed to pull it open just wide enough to let herself in. Inside, it was almost dark. She climbed the narrow stairs and sat down on the bench where—Already it seemed so long ago!—she and Aunt America had sat together.

This bell tower was the one place that she and her aunt had shared alone together. A feeling of comfort welled through her whole body as she sat on the bench.

Now she looked down at the doll lying on her lap. It was a beautiful doll, more beautiful, if possible, than Elena's. She cuddled it, made it sleep and wake up, and examined its clothing.

Yet, though only a short time ago the doll was the thing she wanted most of all in the world, she no longer needed it, she decided. Aunt Lydia had been right: the book was more precious. She would keep the doll nice in the cupboard. Whenever she wanted to, she could take it out and hold it. She smiled to herself in the dusk. And when Anya grew a little older and more careful, she would give the doll to her.